Weird Science

Weird Science

Doug Hawley

Bridge House

British Library Cataloguing in Publication Data
A Record of this Publication is available from the British
Library

ISBN 978-1-914199-40-0

This edition published 2023 by Bridge House Publishing
Manchester, England

Contents

Prime 1

INTERVIEWER: Welcome to the most significant television show ever. I know that it sounds like hyperbole, but this is the first ever interview with our closest relative, sometimes known as a Yeti or abominable snowman.

Because of the worldwide interest, the show is being simulcast around the world in English with translations into every major language with additional showings delayed for prime-time viewing. DVDs will be available within a week of the broadcast.

The first order of business is to introduce our guest on my left. What would you like to be called?

DOOK: A close approximation to my name in human languages would be Dook.

INTERVIEWER: We have so much to learn about you, but why can you speak English?

DOOK: We picked it up from newspapers, radio and television programs which are occasionally in English and from what we call the retrogrades.

INTERVIEWER: It sounds like you must be quick learners. The retrogrades sound interesting, but if you don't mind, I'll get back to them later. I've got so many questions. Legends would have you seven or eight feet tall, but you only appear to be about four and half feet tall, or as non-Americans would say, less than a meter and a half.

DOOK: That's mostly because the people that saw us exaggerated madly. I don't think anyone would claim to be scared by a white furred hobbit.

INTERVIEWER: At least the legends are right about the white fur. I suppose that it helps you live in the cold environment north of India.

DOOK: That's part of it. Do you want the full story?

INTERVIEWER: Absolutely. Our worldwide audience would love all of the details.

DOOK: A few thousand years ago, what you call the yeti, and we call Angwin, or superiors in our language, diverged from homo sapiens. As we evolved to suit our environment, our blood changed to adapt to the altitude. The reason that we are doing this in Nepal is that we Angwin can't thrive in lower altitudes.

Physically, we got smaller with lower metabolism in order to survive on available food sources. Our pelts are much like otters in its insulation. We are usually awake only a few hours a day to conserve energy.

Given our difficult environment, we had to get smarter to survive. We developed edible fungi that thrive in our homes, in tunnels and in caves. I will confess that I personally am not a purist. I've been known to steal food from villages, and grab things left behind by trekkers – they are so wasteful. We are largely vegetarian, but in a pinch...

INTERVIEWER: Your answer invites so many more questions. You seem to imply that you have evolved to be superior to humans.

DOOK: That should be self-evident. We live in harmony, don't pollute and keep our population at a sustainable level.

INTERVIEWER: Relative to your population, I think that our viewers would like to know about your romantic life.

DOOK: Put another way, the drooling viewing perverts want to know about our sex lives. I've seen you glancing at the bulge in my shorts that your producer forced me to wear. Yes, I'm very much a male. Neither males nor females of our species are deficient in any of the ways that trouble our human ancestors and lead to billions in "cures" or "enhancements". Our sex lives are active and inventive. Our flexibility permits acts unimaginable in humans. Better yet, the female easily times births without any artificial methods. In that way, we keep our population stable.

INTERVIEWER: I'm unconvinced about your superiority at this point, but let's talk about the retrogrades that you mentioned earlier.

DOOK: The retrograde story should also convince you of our superiority. Given our relation to humans, every once in a while, we give birth to Angwin that appear human, but have Angwin brains. They act as our emissaries to the unknowing world outside, keeping us up to date on events. Sometimes they just migrate to local villages, and sometimes they travel afar. In fact, some of the villagers know our secret but they have either been discreet, or dismissed as superstitious fools. Many of our retrogrades have been big successes in the world at large. A good example was huge in scientific circles in Switzerland and then the US in the early twentieth century. His equation is known the world around, and improved on the knowledge of a human. An unfortunate example of ours was a very rich man in the US who went into politics, but at least he succeeded. Our take is that he was corrupted by long exposure to human society.

INTERVIEWER: Is the North American bigfoot or sasquatch related to you?

DOOK: We frankly believe that the bigfoot stories are myths, despite the widely circulated photo of Doug Hawley with a purported bigfoot in Oregon.

INTERVIEWER: One last question for what I hope that will be one of many interviews. Why are you talking to us now after previously being so shy?

DOOK: It may be a vain hope, but we are hoping to halt an

8

encroaching human population. There is no way that I can be diplomatic – we want nothing that humans have to offer, and we don't want to be overrun or exploited. We hope to form a coalition to allow us a homeland, something like Israel, but without the continuous conflict.

Better Living Through Electronics

1

We are playing LA. Since LA beat us in the finals last year, it's always great to beat them. I would not be surprised if we meet them in the finals this year. No question, we will win in four. Tonight, we are playing in LA. Clearly, the game will be decided at the end.

No surprise, we are down a point with ten seconds to go and we have the ball. I think that we have the best point guard in the NBA. Will Jackson is third in the NBA in assists, gets a few rebounds and scores in double digits. At 6'5" he has either height or speed on every opposing guard. Stan Novack, a Polish import, starts at small forward. Damn fast for a white man, and holds his own by doing the little things – setting picks, getting some rebounds and playing good team D. Our shooting guard, Steve Goodman is two years out of high school and fifth in the league in scoring. He doesn't do much else, but the rest of us handle everything else. Center Keith Daniels is a 7'4" center from Brigham Young. He is so white, he is almost invisible, but he is tops in the league in blocked shots and fourth in rebounds. He doesn't have much shooting range, but unlike Shaq, he is an 80% free throw shooter, so he gets his share of close in shots and dunks as well as making lots of free throws. The bench? Well, the bench is what management could afford after paying for our superb starting lineup – some guys on the way down, some on the way up, and some who were available.

Oh, yeah that leaves the power forward, ME. James (not Jim or Jimmy) Jones. Based on my size, a lot of people think of me as the next Shaq. No way. Shaq used to tell Karl Malone not to take his shirt off in the locker room because Karl was so ripped. Based on my physique and the way I play (except for not hurting so many other players), I think that I am the natural successor to Mr. Malone as THE power forward of my generation. Tim Duncan and Kevin Garnett are good, but they are at the end of their careers, and I'm the future. Don't believe, look at the numbers. No brag, just facts.

I know that I said there were just ten seconds left, how can I be saying all this? Times like this, things slow down. It's relativity or something that I can't explain. Will drives, but is covered on the way to the basket, so he kicks the ball out to Steve. My man turns his head, Steve makes one of his rare passes in to me, and I dunk. If the backboards weren't reinforced, it would have shattered. Thunder and lighting, man.

Three seconds on the clock. LA takes their time out. Being LA, most of the crowd has left. They get the ball to Kobe, Keith stuffs him, game over.

Back to the hotel, feeling good. Much as I hate LA as a city and as an NBA team, I love the women, and the feeling is mutual. Most of the team get their pick of the women, but Keith is a married straight arrow and Steve, well we wonder about Steve. I try to alternate the races as an affirmative action kind of guy. White – black – white – black – whose turn is it? Holy Moses, think I'll have Chinese tonight. She's big – maybe 5'10" and built like a porn queen with a beautiful porcelain skin.

Got myself a winner. We discussed life before, during and after. She had rebelled against her parents and wishes to marry a nice Chinese boy. While in college she developed a taste for black athletes. She is pretty athletic herself. Obviously studied the Kama Sutra. She is currently a college professor in English lit. She is widely traveled and very sophisticated.

2

Horace Cram cleared 5' – barely. His moustache was visible – barely. Legs – hairless. Charisma – none. Intelligence – fairly high about unimportant things. All this in a pear-shaped package. His bifocals make him look like an illustration of a nerd in an encyclopedia. Imagine a short, even uglier Bill Gates. Behind his back, people joked about his assberger's syndrome – a play on the word for a high performing autistic. By a stroke of fortune, he also had some of a nerd's ability at electrical engineering and is employed testing new media products at Electrowiz. He has hopes that his stock would explode with Electrowiz's new product.

"Hey Jane, join me for coffee."

"Sorry, Horace I've got a ton of work and can't leave my desk. No time to talk, no time to walk."

Jane is 3" taller than Horace before the puts on her heels, makes more than he does, is classically attractive without trying, in short way out of his league. She has turned him down ten times, but Horace rations his attentions so as not be in the total obsessive stalker mold.

Horace does a quick calculation and decides he can ask about an after-work beer in two weeks.

3

We are jamming in Cleveland. I know, I know, I know. Cleveland. But we are always out of our heads in Cleveland. Out of body, out of mind. Crazy. We are tighter when we should be tight, looser when we should be loose.

As always, we are mixing it up. Segues are for kids or the anal retentive. We switch from our Afro-Cuban signature "TimbucHavana2" to our "Honky Tonk Women" cover. More horns on the former, more guitar on the latter. Got to have our swing medley later. Hot lights, hotter music. We are all virtuosos, but my name and piano lead the way.

I'm Gonzales. People like to guess about me. I think that a little mystery is a good thing. I'm from Cuba, but my Ingles is pretty good. I picked up a good university education along the way. Although I have stuck with music all the way, my curiosity led me into courses on physics, literature and politics. With my shaved head, brown goatee and light brown skin my "race" is unclear to my fans. It is to me as well, but I suspect there are some African, European and Indio in there.

I grab a saxophone. I only do this when I'm really feeling good. It is time to cover Ray's "The Nighttime is the Right Time". We learned so much from him, I wish he were still around. We could, and have, played Ray all night. There were a few months after he died when we did nothing but tributes. The good stuff, not much of the Country stuff (some exceptions – "I'm Movin' On" and "You Are My Sunshine"). We worked with "Drown In My own Tears", "Hard Times" and "Tell the Truth". We had to augment our backup vocals, but we had some great singers along.

After a little experimentation with mind-bending drug and drink, I've limited myself to a couple of drinks a night. Despite what I thought I was doing after grass or coke, the recordings always showed that the band sucked. I've had to can a few players, who would not walk the line, but we are the better for it, and I don't want to be an enabler. Being sober allows the band to do something different than any other group that I know – we go for a short run or walk after our final set. This has cut us off from some who think that a popular band has to be into weird stuff, but it works for us and has connected us to a lot of fans who might not otherwise notice us. We move to some Santana covers, some old Fats Domino, and close with the obscure, but stone groove "Goin' Home Tomorrow" by Little Richard. We get a lot of love from the audience before we take off for the Big Apple tomorrow.

4

Horace is not connecting with humans. Maybe a cat would help his loneliness. If a cat worked, he might work his way up to a dog. If not, he could retreat to an amphibian or reptile of some sort.

A trip to the pound gives him plenty of alternatives. First, he eliminates the aloof cats. He has had enough of that with people. He finally picks two sisters so they can entertain each other while he is at work.

The cat thing turns out pretty well. Caring for the cats distracts Horace somewhat from his dismal waking hours and gives him something to do besides his work. The two tabbies have intriguingly different personalities. The orange one, Sherry, grows a lot and is very placid and clingy. The black one, Beelzebub (usually Bub), is wiry, loud and independent. Bub tries to run the whole house.

The cats are working, maybe he can try people again.

5

Pretty damn good for a small-town boy from Springfield. In my second term as U. S. Senator, I'm given credit for balancing the budget and bringing peace to much of the world. There that seems to be little question Joe Jackson, (great political name and what is on my birth certificate) will be the next president. The incumbent, that hypocritical, incompetent Samuel Dyer probably won't run again. He has so discredited the Repubs with his deficits and his foreign wars right out of "Wag the Dog" that they will probably run some sacrificial lamb even crazier than he is. Dick Cheney has been mentioned and he hasn't been out of the hospital for six months. The only democrat talking about running against me is Hillary and she is so unpopular that Dyer beat her last time around. The idiot war criminal Bush is being asked not to say anything for fear of cutting out the last few Republican members of congress.

After Dyer won by the slimmest of margins, the Republicans had completely run out of gas. They would have been better off to have lost because as the opposition they would have had some support. When Dyer started to talk about invading Iran, he lost almost all of his dwindling support. The few Republicans left in congress after the midterm elections wouldn't even support him. Business was hurting so bad from the Republican deficits, they told him to raise taxes. He is now a sick, beaten fifty-five year old man who seemed so young and strong just two years ago. He was the Republican John Kennedy in terms of charm. Now he is the stupid, ugly Ted Kennedy of Republicans.

The public wanted a new voice. Hillary was a loser. The rest of the pack was old, old, old news and tied to unpopular interest groups or ideas. Joe Jackson the previously unknown is in the right place at the right time.

The public was finally ready to quit the Republican imperialism, but it was my legislation that reduced military expenditures to those of the European Union. My legislation got our troops out of the Far East, the Middle East and Europe. If South Korea did not want us there, why should we be there?

Rationing medicine was very unpopular at first, but when the public learned the percent of expenditures on people 80 and up, and for babies that would never have much of a life; I was able to push through laws limiting payments for lost causes. We will save billions.

With these political breakthroughs, my plans for reforming energy and cutting the trade deficit as a consequence are eagerly awaited. I'm John McCain, only much better. It's hard to be humble, but I have to work on it for the news conferences.

6

Horace says his work on Dream Ware is ready for Beta testing. There are hundreds of male nerds and fat chicks lined up for testing. To make it simple, the first version has a short menu for directed dreaming:

Sports star
    Football
    Soccer
    Tennis
    Baseball
    Basketball
    Cricket (only outside the Americas)

Politics
    Senator
    Representative
    President
    Prime Minister (non-US)

Entertainer
    Singer
    Musician
    Actor
    Celebrity
    Rehab

The usual gender and orientations choices

If the tests are successful, Electrowiz expects to sell 500 million units for $3,000 each at a profit of $500 million. Horace is given a $10 million bonus and allowed to work his own hours. "Total Recall", at least during dreaming, is now an affordable reality rather than science fiction, but most users don't look like Arnold Schwarzenegger in his prime.

7

The next day Jane asks Horace out for coffee. He gladly accepts. During the coffee date, Horace says to Jane, "You know, you are looking really good today. May I take your picture?" Jane says, "Sure."

As they go back to work, Jane tells Horace, "Say, why don't we see each other outside work?" Horace says, "I'll have to check my schedule, but I'll see you in my dreams."

8

In the future, Horace only shows up for work about three hours a day, saying that he's working on something at home. He avoids Jane and buys a lot of sleeping pills.

Appeared in *Potluck* and *Wilderness House*

Prime 2

JULIE COLLINS: This is Julie Collins back with our second interview with Dook, the representative of the Yeti, or as they say, the Angwin.

JULIE COLLINS: What has happened since I last talked to you? I know that you wanted to get agreement on an Angwin homeland.

DOOK: There have been bumps along the way, but we never thought that it would be easy. We share with humans the idea that we should hope for the best, expect the worst. We've made little obvious progress towards our goal, and there have been threats against us, mostly against me. We know that we will prevail however.

JULIE COLLINS: Are you doing something to protect yourself and your people?

DOOK: Yes, but I'll get to that later.

JULIE COLLINS: You are not physically imposing. Do you have heavy weapons at your disposal?

DOOK: I'd rather not say. We don't want to give our enemies too much information.

JULIE COLLINS: Can you give us the specifics of various nations' response to your proposal?

DOOK: I mentioned one of our retrogrades in the first interview. He is now the president of a powerful country. His response was highly negative:

"I've cast my lot with the humans and renounce the sad yeti people. You are small in all ways. It would be against our interest to grant you any sovereignty. With the rapid climate change, there may come a time when iron, coal and even gold may be mined where you live. I want the opportunity to extract whatever lies under your land. If that means that you must move, we can just set you up in North Dakota. It ought to look like

18

home to you and I could use more workers on the pipeline."

That was the formal response, which had more than 140 characters. Shortly thereafter, we received a tweet. "I might reconsider if you would introduce me to some of the yeti women."

JULIE COLLINS: How about your neighbors?

DOOK: That was not a surprise at all. Most if not all of the countries in our region are concerned about giving up a square centimeter of land, regardless of its value. India, Pakistan, China, Nepal all have been arguing over the extent of their territory. Each turned us down flat. The Tibet representative said that he would be glad to negotiate after Tibet got home rule, which isn't likely to happen unless the China government changes.

JULIE COLLINS: And other countries?

DOOK: Most of them are in favor of our home rule, which is easy to understand. I can't imagine that what happens here would affect Uruguay at all, so they get to play the good guys at no cost.

JULIE COLLINS: So, does all of this that mean that you give up?

DOOK: Not at all. I mentioned the retrogrades in our last interview. They are Angwin mutants with brains like Angwin, bodies like humans. It is odd that those who have seen me on TV are perfectly willing to accept the existence of normal Angwin, but not our retrogrades. Those who oppose us seem to have forgotten that the retrogrades with their superior intelligence and human looks can support our cause without being detected.

The water supply in several major cities in countries that oppose us have experienced a barely detectible sweetness in their water supply – Beijing, Mumbai and Chicago to name a few. The little bit of sugar in the water caused no harm, but what if our retrogrades had put something else in the water? The rulers in the countries that are against us should think about the possibilities. We have no interest in causing harm, but we insist on what is owed to us.

We will get our homeland. Those that signed on early will receive the benefit of our agricultural and medical secrets which will greatly aid their societies. Those that acquiesce later lose.

JULIE COLLINS: I'm pleased to hear of your future success. What else has been happening?

DOOK: There are organizations that want to attack our territory on either speciest or aggressive grounds. It shouldn't be necessary to repeat that they cannot depend on any of their members not to be double agents. Additionally, our homes are nigh impregnable, and we have efficient weapons. Suffice to say – save yourself a lot of blood and forget it. Further, anyone attempting to make good on threats on my life is as good as dead.

A very sad note is the interest in displaying one of us as the "Hottentot Venus" that was done a century ago. If you don't know about that shameful spectacle, I suggest that you look it up. To be clear, we do not take part in any degrading demonstration for any amount of money.

JULIE COLLINS: You mention "speciest". What do you consider yourselves?

DOOK: We are "homo angwin". Same questionable genus name, but different species.

JULIE COLLINS: You've revealed some very dangerous schemes. Is there any good news?

DOOK: Since our interview, I've been in touch with Doug Hawley who has the famous sasquatch photo. He has convinced me that it is legitimate.

JULIE COLLINS: Anything else?

DOOK: I have some very good news. While we have no interest in exploitation, I have a great singing voice in both pure Angwin and Western styles. My versions of '60s songs like "Roll With It" and "Sledgehammer" put the originals to shame. My agent can be reached at 503-555-1234 in Lake Oswego Oregon.

JULIE COLLINS: Despite the power of this interview, I fear that we must quit for now. No time for closing statements or questions from the audience. I hope that everyone comes back for our next interview when we can talk about the Angwin homeland. This will be rebroadcast and DVDs are available.

Appeared in *Occulum*

Soul

All of the following news articles appeared in the Daily Northwest News.

February 10, 2043 Copenhagen, Denmark

Using new detection equipment built by Nobel Prize winner in physics **Magnus Albreck, Frank Smelling** and the staff at the National Physics Laboratory have discovered electromagnetic waves previously detected nowhere in the universe. The wavelength of these newly discovered waves is shorter than any previously observed.

The discovery excited physicists around the world. At this time, the source of the waves is unknown and there has been no independent verification of **Albreck**'s and **Smelling**'s results. The practical use of the results is unknown at this time.

February 27, 2043 Copenhagen, Denmark

In a follow up to an earlier discovery, Magnus Albreck and associates at the Denmark National Physics Lab have identified the source of previously unrecorded electromagnetic waves originally discovered in late 2042. The waves originated from lab technician **Helga Stein**. Stein was in close proximity to measuring device, Extended EMW, when the waves first registered. Whenever no one was close to the Extended EMW, no S (for **Stein**) waves were recorded. Subsequent experiments recorded S waves for other laboratory personnel with slightly differing wave lengths and amplitudes.

March 1, 2043 Nashville, TN

Chester Ogilvie, leader of Baptist USA claims that Danish scientists have discovered the human soul. After years of religious and spiritual claims to a distinctly human soul as an unmeasured driving force in all humans, he sees the S waves discovered at the Denmark National Physics Lab in late 2042 as proof of the soul's existence. "They have not found S waves anywhere but in humans, so I think that it is obvious that the human soul has finally been quantified. Those who have never taken religion seriously now have scientific proof that we uniquely have souls and are not just more atoms in a materialistic universe."

Neither **Magnus Albreck** nor **Frank Smelling** of the Denmark Lab were immediately available for comment. **Bhati Nempali** of the Halide Institute of Chicago responded that "a new form of electromagnetic wave may have been discovered. The Danish Lab work has not been peer reviewed at this time. Whatever they discovered is just another physical phenomenon, not the basis for superstitious claptrap."

March 3, 2043 Chicago

Professor **Bhati Nempali** of the Halide Institute of Chicago, who two days ago questioned the nature of S waves, and indirectly cast aspersion on religious leader **Chester Ogilvie** of Baptist USA in Nashville, TN, apologized saying, "In my earlier remarks I did not intend to offend anyone of any religious belief." Mr. **Nempali**'s contract with the Halide is up later this year and congressional hearings are scheduled next month on Federal research funding.

March 5, 2043 Interactive Listing

Today at 5PM on Channel IA4322: **Daytona Brown** will moderate a chat with guest experts on the S waves. Are they real? Do only people have them? Are they a manifestation of the soul? Are there any commercial applications?

Daytona Brown – Let me introduce the participants. We are honored to have the discoverer of S waves, **Magnus Albreck**, imminent theologian **Chester Ogilvie, Jeremy Atkins** of PETA, abortions rights supporter **Sue Feldman** and biologist and well-known atheist **Roger Sawkins**. Do you have opening statements?

Albreck – First, let me spread the credit around. The waves were discovered coming from **Helga Stein**, a very important colleague. Many at the Danish National Lab have worked on the equipment that did the recording. I'm just the first among equals. Second, we have lots of work to do before we can draw hard conclusions.

Ogilvie – I say it is not too early to draw conclusions. Do S waves come from coffee cans? Do they come from lab rats? No, I don't think so. Despite some of the negatives I have heard, we have evidence of the human soul. Now, I'm not saying my particular brand of religion has all the answers, but I think that Professor **Albreck**'s work has proven that there is a spiritual plane of existence beyond the physical.

Feldman – Before anyone suggests that this in anyway invalidates abortion rights, let me remind everyone that some abortions may still be best for society and for women who are not prepared to give birth.

Atkins – If we have a spiritual existence, I think that we will find that our animal brothers are on the same plane and deserve the same respect that humans deserve. We need to test chimps, dogs, cats and other animals to see if they have S waves.

Sawkins – Let's go back to what Professor **Albreck** said. It is too early to draw conclusions. Can we all just keep an open mind and go by what is proven rather than conjectured.

Brown – Hypothetically, let us say that S waves are exclusive to humans. What does that mean?

Ogilvie – Why, clearly, we will have scientific proof that man is God's crowning achievement and is uniquely suited for a heavenly paradise after death.

Feldman – It doesn't change anything for me.

Albreck – From the point of view of physics, I don't think that we are prepared to conclude anything.

Sawkins – I agree that we will not know exactly why only humans have S waves, if that is in fact correct, but I could suggest that it relates to some unique human feature. There are subtle, but real differences between the human brain and those of other animals.

Atkins – Regardless of the presence or absence of S waves in non-human animals, I think that all animals deserve our respect. In fact, if indeed we are different from our animal brother, that implies that we should show them the treatment that our greater consciousness allows us.

Brown – How has the discovery of S waves changed any of your opinions?

Sawkins – I am now open to the belief that humans are a unique form of animal.

Albreck – I am just amazed at the progress we are making in understanding ourselves and our universe. I did not think that this big a discovery would be made in my lifetime.

Ogilvie – A lot of people, including myself, have thought that science and religion were at odds. We now have a case where science is now clearly supporting religion.

Atkins – I now accept the possibility that humans may be unique, but it does not change in any way my opinion about the treatment of animals.

Feldman – The existence of S waves convinces me more than ever that we need to do research on the physical and emotional aspects of abortions and find ways to make most of them unnecessary. Much as we eliminated smoking, we have the technology to avoid unwanted pregnancies. I would much rather stop unwanted pregnancies than debate abortion.

Brown – Closing statements?

Ogilvie – I hope all of those who have rejected religion in their lives are now open to the real possibility that they were mistaken.

Atkins – Whether we are the equals or stewards of non-human animals, they deserve our respect and humane treatment.

Albreck – I think that we have just scratched the surface of S wave research, and I look forward to continued research and new revelations.

Sawkins – I hope that the physics research from the Danish National Physics Lab is married with biological research to fully explore the implications of S waves.

Brown – I think that this discussion has just started, but we are out of time. Perhaps we can reconvene in a year and talk about progress in the study of S waves. For now, I'd like to thank all of the participants for a respectful and insightful panel on the beginning of a new era.

The following news article appeared in the Daily Northwest News.

March 15, 2044 Copenhagen, Denmark

A little over a year ago, S waves were discovered at the National Physics Laboratory by Magnus Albreck. Originally, they were only detected in humans, leading some to claim that they were a physical manifestation of soul. We just received news that weak S waves have been discovered in chimps.

The same panel that discussed the original discovery has been reconvened to discuss this revelation.

Daytona Brown – As we indicated during the panel of March 5, 2043 which I led, we are now having the follow up discussion of S waves. The timing is great because of the news that S waves have been found in chimps.

We have a panel with some of the original members and some new ones. Unfortunately, **Chester Ogilvie**, leader of Baptist USA died recently and abortion supporter Sue Feldman is unavailable, but we have **Jason Evans** of the Los Angeles Universalist Church and **Mary Proctor** from Planned Parenthood to replace them. Biologist and atheist **Roger Sawkins, Magnus Albreck** the discoverer of the S Waves and **Jeremy Atkins** from PETA are back from last year's panel.

Brown – Opening Statements?

Evans – I don't know how Mr. **Ogilvie** would have felt about these results. Maybe that there are many mansions in the Lord's heaven? Chimp mansions and human mansions? I don't think that these waves necessarily represent soul, but I'm keeping an open mind.

Sawkins – No matter how many animals or objects give off S waves, I don't believe in God or heaven. However, finding another source of S waves is intriguing.

Proctor – This has no effect on me. We don't get much call for chimp abortions.

Atkins – I think that we have more evidence that higher apes are our brothers and sisters and should be treated with respect equal to humans. In fact, that respect should be accorded to all non-human animals.

Albreck – I was amazed at the discovery of S waves in humans. Now that they exist in at least some animals, I wonder what we will find tomorrow.

Brown – In what way do these later results affect your thinking?

Sawkins – Before when S waves were only found in humans, I believed that there was a qualitative difference between humans and animals. Now I have to questions that. What will we find with more sensitive machines?

Evans – We Universalists are divided about a supreme being. If we can identify S waves as representing the soul, I believe that will tip the debate.

Proctor – Until S waves are confirmed to exist in fetuses, I think that the majority of the

US will still favor allowing abortions as now permitted by the law. If S waves are found in the fetus, we have a whole new ballgame.

Atkins – It doesn't change my thinking at all, it confirms what I thought all along.

Albreck – It makes we want to see if we can refine our EMW machinery to find any S waves anywhere else, perhaps with lower amplitude than those presently detectable.

Brown – Closing statements?

Proctor – Regardless of whom or what has S waves, let's use science and education to keep abortions safe and rare.

Evans – Whether or not you believe in God, any person or animal with S waves is special.

Atkins – I concur with Mr. **Evans**.

Albreck – I'll be back in the lab. I'm elated to be living in these times with the progress we're making.

Sawkins – I hope that Dr. **Albreck** will collaborate with my fellow biologists to see what the implication of S waves is in the animals that have them.

First published: "Soul 1" in *Wi-Files* (closed), "Soul 2" in *Oblong* (closed). Combined in *Down In The Dirt*.

Dark

Stan invited her to lunch to talk about Dark Hill.

Stan said, "I just happen to know their head of personnel. Let's go talk to him."

Jackie responded, "Don't you mean human resources?"

"One of the things that I like about the Dark Hill execs is that they are dinosaurs like me. No 'human resources', 'people of color', 'issues' or 'Baker City' for us. We think that the language that we used twenty years ago worked just fine. Somebody dying of cancer doesn't have 'health issues' for god's sake, he has a health problem. If the town is 'Hood River' in Hood River County, why can't 'Baker City' in Baker County still be 'Baker'?"

Jackie tended to agree with Stan, but she kept quiet because Stan's rants could go on for half an hour if encouraged.

Stan seemed to catch Jackie's attitude and moved on. "The two of us will have lunch with their guy Will James next Friday and see if he has any ideas. I'll clear it with Jane."

They met in the Dark Hill cafeteria. Will greeted them with, "What a good-looking couple of white people. How are you today and who is this beauty you brought with you?" Jackie was a little surprised to see a black man in a largely white industry in largely white Bend.

"We are good Will. Jackie is one of our ace statisticians and you are definitely a good-looking example of your race."

The guys laughed a lot, but Jackie couldn't help feeling a little uncomfortable. Later she understood that it was their silly guy stuff.

"Here's the deal, Will. Jackie applied her advanced mathematics skills to find out that your health claims record

32

is way better than average the last year, but couldn't find any explanation. She tried similar employee groups and groups for your region. We matched demographics. In every case Dark Hill aced everyone else by a large margin. So we are here to find out what you are doing right."

"That is a puzzler. Personally, I'm very healthy as you no doubt know, because I clean your clock every time that we go one on one on the basketball court. Not only that, but the girls always want me to be skins. I hadn't thought about it before, but I do think that we are trending down on sick days. Right now, I can't think of anything that's changed in the last year that would change our claims stats, but I'll give it a little more thought. Maybe I'll need to let you know in person. How is the fishing around Wilsonville?"

"I'll need to find out before you visit."

"I might show up sooner if all of the statisticians at Healthion look like Jackie."

"We are getting on troubling grounds, as somebody in human resources, I mean personnel, should know. It could be actionable harassment if I told you that Jackie is by far our best-looking statistician."

Jackie worked at keeping a straight face.

On the way back to Wilsonville Jackie asked, "How do you know Will so well?"

"We were fraternity brothers at U of O and both of us were a couple of give a shit jokers, so we naturally bonded together against the tight-asses. Plus, we both liked our dads' music – Little Richard, Everly Brothers, Ray Charles and like that and were crazy about the Trail Blazers. He's married, so I can't fix him you up with him, but I can set you up with one of his unmarried brothers."

"No thanks."

"Don't like black guys or do you prefer girls?"

"None of your damned business, but I usually date guys

and I've dated guys from every recognized ethnic group and some others that only I know about."

"Sorry about my insensitivity, but I've got a mental disability – I'm a guy. How about broken hearts?"

"So far theirs seven and mine five, so I'm up two on the scoreboard. Right now I'm in play."

It occurred to both of them that it had gotten a little too personal and they didn't say anything for the next half hour but pretended to watch Smith Rocks north of Bend and then the trees on US26 east of Mt. Hood.

Stan broke the ice with, "So aren't you too bright for your position at Healthion? Not that I'm suggesting you leave."

"Short answer, yes, I am too bright for my position at Healthion. Longer answer, it requires so little of my mind that I can work on my poetry and math games in my head while I'm at work."

Stan just gawped in response to her revelation. He hoped he didn't look as stupid as he felt.

"My turn. Since we are getting personal, how long ago were you and Will at the U of O."

"About mumble years ago."

"You really just said mumble in place of a number?"

"Yeah, you would never believe the actual number because I look sooo much younger."

Jackie snorted and some snot came out of her nose, and then they were both guffawing out of control. Rather than being grossed out, Stan was enchanted.

At that point in the trip, they felt so comfortable with each other that they started to run scenarios internally. Jackie thought he's got to be married or gay and Stan thought there has to be some rule about dating a fellow employee.

They were both wrong.

Three weeks after the trip to Dark Hill, Will called up to ask about the fishing around Wilsonville. Stan said, "No idea, but why don't you come up here and I'll take you to Wankers Corner which has good beer and all the free peanuts that you can eat. Is this just personal, or do you have an answer about your health claims?"

"Before I answer your question, I have one. Does wanker mean the same thing in Wilsonville that it does in Britain?"

"I've wondered that for years. I suspect it means something different in Wilsonville. Probably named after Franklin Wanker, or something like that."

"OK, I'll answer your question. I have an idea why our claims are so low, but you probably won't believe it. Anyway, I want you to take me to dinner and hang out. You know Wilsonville isn't that far from Bend, buddy."

"Damn straight, we don't see enough of each other, brother from a different mother."

"Stan, please cut out the cheese."

"OK, that was overboard."

The next day Will got into Wilsonville and stored some overnight stuff at Stan's place. Will refused to answer questions about business until they got to Wankers Corner, started on their first beer and shelled some peanuts.

"OK, spill. Now."

"I see they don't serve any Dark Hill Stout here. The customers are in line for a lot of health problems."

"Huh?"

"OK, be as skeptical as you want. After racking my brain and asking around the brewery, I was reminded that we started to send a monthly case of beer home with all the employees a year and a half ago. It was cheaper than raises, and it made for happy workers, sometimes too happy. That is the only thing that changed at the time our loss ratio improved. You need to start charging us less for health coverage."

Without commenting on cheaper health coverage, Stan said, "So beer drinkers are healthier? I have a hard time believing that."

"First, it's not just any beer, its dark beer. More specifically, it is the Dark Hill Stout, the one that we send home with them."

"Well, yeah I'm skeptical until we can do more research."

"I'm good with that. Let's have another round of this unhealthy beer."

After they started their second, Will asked, "Are you still hanging out with those bimbos since Joyce left?"

"Don't start."

"Listen, you do know that they are seeing you for your stash. Worse, they could give you the gift that keeps discharging."

"Hey, I'm a big boy now; I know about condoms."

"Here's what I find troubling. You are working with a beautiful and bright woman. I'm talking about Jackie. Anything going on there? Oh, so you can still blush."

"It must be my Irish. I have to use SPF 1000 outdoors. Look, she's a co-worker, there are ethical considerations."

"Just in case you don't remember, I'm head of personnel at Dark Hill. There is probably no problem if you are not in the same chain of command."

Stan considered that and answered. "No, we are parallel in the organization. Not that I'm considering a romance."

"Sure you're not."

"I don't know how you can use my explanation for the good health at Dark Hill, but I'm going to put our chemists on it and see if they can find out if our beer is different somehow. I see another Nobel prize in it for me."

"Another Nobel prize?"

"I got my first one when I disconnected my door bell."

"Arghh – more drink, less talk."

Meanwhile Stan didn't know that Jackie had already checked around and found out that Stan was divorced and very heterosexual, but she didn't want to make the first move.

Just to be sure, Stan checked with his personnel department and found out that strictly hypothetically he could date Jackie. Given the possibility of a healthy relationship, he realized how miserable that he had been since Joyce left him "to find herself". A part of "finding herself" involved a poetry professor at Portland State. Under his tutelage, she is trying to get her self-involved poetic treasures published.

With the decks cleared, they approached each other cautiously like two porcupines. It started with lunches together at work, progressed to hikes and picnics and went to weekends at either his or her place. Without any formal announcement, they became recognized as a couple.

After some phone conversations Will and Stan realized that even though they had been best friends in college, it had been a year between their last visit and Stan's business trip to Bend. For years after college, they had been close, but they had gone their own ways for some time. Will assumed, correctly, that some of their estrangement had been caused by Stan's turmoil with Joyce. Stan had felt so betrayed and guilty about Joyce's racism, that he felt awkward around Will even after Joyce left him. Joyce would give unsubtle hints like "Can't you find better friends?"

Stan insisted, "It's about 150 miles; we got to trade visits at least once a month."

"OK, you come to my place first."

"OK if I bring Jackie?"

"Listen, I am so happy that you have started making some good decisions, even though it is late in your life."

"Are you still claiming that we were friends in college when you were there ten years ago, and I was there twenty years ago even though the math doesn't work?"

"How wrong can I be when everyone believes me?"

"So how about I show up Friday evening in a couple of weeks? Maybe you'll be able to explain your miracle elixir by then."

"It's a plan. Jody will barbeque and you will be expected to entertain the kids."

At Will's place, Jackie joyfully took over entertaining the kids; leading Stan to wonder why Jackie hadn't already married and started a family. Before dismissing the thought as presumptuous, he thought, *Better for me.*

Left to talk business and drink beer, Will led with, "It's the terroir."

Before Will could say anything else, Stan said, "That's wine talk, isn't it?"

"I can see that you are in for an education. Dark beers are bitter because they are very 'hoppy' and hops depend on the climate and soil in which they are grown. Our research staff has found out that the fields around Hubbard where our hops are grown have unique properties that may not be found anywhere else. It has unusual proportions of selenium, copper and other trace elements, probably from volcanic eruptions. It also contains some organic compounds that we have not identified yet. The unique soil produces unique hops. We can't explain the health benefits yet, but the staff swears that our hops are the reason for them. It is possible that other dark beers may also convey some health benefits."

Stan and Will went about their business, exchanging

visits over the next several months. Stan and Jackie became as much a couple as Will and Jody. At one of the visits Will was all smiles. "We presented all the stats that we have along with the analysis of the hops and now all of those government alphabets – FDA and so on, will allow us to make legitimate health claims for Dark Hill Stout. Our analysis of competitive dark beers indicates that they have some of the healthy ingredients that we have, but not all. Of course, we won't tell them that; they'll have to find out for themselves. In the meantime, we will boost our production of our stout as much as possible while continuing to be a craft brewery. We have quietly bought up some land with similar makeup to our original supplier, so we can get a lot more hops."

"Are you sure that the public will go for it?"

"I've been talking to newspaper and TV medical columnists. They are buying in. Believe me, this will be huge. But wait there is more – I've been checking our employee records and the divorce rate is way below expected. I think that our stout makes people happier as well as healthier."

"Couldn't it be that any beer makes people happier?"

"Stan, you know better than that. Heavy drinkers have much higher rates of depression and divorce. For whatever reason, we think that our stout drinkers quit after drinking just enough to elevate their mood, but not enough to be roaring drunk."

Back in Wilsonville, a very nervous Stan said to Jackie, "Listen, I don't want to spend any more of my life being single. You are the one, please marry me. I want to start a family now."

Jackie, who had wondered if Stan would ever get around to asking, wasted no time saying yes.

Will was the best man at the wedding and Jackie's

sisters and Jody were bridesmaids. They kept it small, because Jackie had no interest in spectacles and Stan remembered the aftermath of the huge, expensive wedding to Joyce.

A month later Jackie was expecting and she and Stan were overjoyed.

Dark Hill had found a way to make a hop supplement, which didn't taste too good, but had most of the health and happiness effects of the beer. Now teetotalers and those that didn't want to stay buzzed continuously could reap the benefits of Dark Hill Stout.

Dark Hill was rolling in money and the employees' profit-sharing plan made them rich. Tourists flocked to Bend to visit the brewery and many stayed. The introduction of Dart Hill Stout by an industrial brewer in New Jersey, with a label which was almost the same as Dark Hill Stout was a small wrinkle, but the Dark Hill lawyers handled that quickly.

Jackie gave birth to a healthy Andy and eleven months later to an equally healthy Sandra.

Will called Stan a couple of years after the discovery of the wonders of Dark Hill Stout. "One thing that we didn't study earlier is that the stout doubles fertility. As with all the other properties, we know what happens, but not why."

Two years after Jackie originally noticed the superb claims ratio at Dark Hill, syndicated columnist Jason Atkins wrote a column "The 'Dark Ages' Are A New Golden Age" in response to the improved mental and physical health of the US caused by Dark Hill Stout and Dark Hill Pills.

After five years of peace and prosperity the Federal Office Of Budget and Management announced that the standard of living in the United States would be cut in half in fifteen years due to the burgeoning costs of educating the increasing number of students and social security for seniors who were living ten year longer.

———————————

Published in *Potluck* (closed) and *Commuter Lit*

Prime 3

JULIE COLLINS: We are here for the third interview with Yeti/Angwin spokesman.

DOOK. For the five people living under rocks in Blankistan, in the first two interviews we learned that the Angwin are small relatives of humans, who live in the Himalayas. They sometimes have mutant progeny that look just like humans, but all of them are brilliant. Dook agreed to an interview in order to gain a homeland for his people. After a few troubles, he has succeeded and he will tell you about that today.

JULIE COLLINS: Tell us Dook, how you succeeded.

DOOK: We always knew that we would prevail. As you know from the last interview, we used the stick of mass sabotage to recalcitrant nations and the carrot of our advanced knowledge. Almost all nations fell into line.

JULIE COLLINS: There were exceptions?

DOOK: Yes, but I won't name them. There are a number of failed states that have no functioning government and therefore can neither accept nor reject us. One nation, once considered the most powerful, has become an international pariah and has no interests outside its border. The lack of acceptance from those places is irrelevant.

JULIE COLLINS: Where do you go from here?

DOOK: We are currently setting up boundaries and working on limited trade. We intend to export technology and knowledge and import some food we can't produce and some electronics. Based on stories from our mutants, the retrogrades, we'd probably enjoy TV such as *The Venture Brothers* and *Playing House*, and music from Neil Young and Jerry Lee Lewis.

JULIE COLLINS: Do you have a government in place to deal with the outside world?

DOOK: We have a representative council, with rotating members, which votes on issues that concern us. That's how we came up with the plan for a homeland.

JULIE COLLINS: No president, prime minister or grand poobah?

DOOK: Don't have any, don't need any.

JULIE COLLINS: But surely you have some exalted position in that you speak for the Angwin.

DOOK: I drew the short straw. Some others have been chosen to speak to various audiences around the world that are curious about us. We can also experience other cultures that way.

JULIE COLLINS: Won't you be affected by lower elevations?

DOOK: One of the retrogrades has invented a device that limits our oxygen, something like the opposite of portable oxygen that your people with limited lung capacity use. If you think we look strange now, you should see us wearing that appliance. Yetis from space!

JULIE COLLINS: Do you have allies or alliances?

DOOK: Alliances lead to war and other forms of insanity. We don't need to be in the United Nations, NATO, ASEAN. Having our homeland is enough. Although we can defend ourselves as has been proven, we will avoid conflict.

JULIE COLLINS: Anything else that you would like to share before we finish up?

DOOK: I brought enough Tibetan Peach Pie for you and the studio audience.

JULIE COLLINS: Thanks from me and the audience. I hope that we can talk again soon.

Appeared in *Occulum*

Cats' Religion

One lazy Saturday afternoon, our fat orange cat Kitzhaber climbed on to my lap while I was relaxing in my Lazy Boy. The cat is named after our governor because the cat wouldn't make a good governor either. I woke up later from a dream in which Kitzhaber said, "I don't like what you call me. Why would anyone want to be named after a governor that resigned in disgrace? Call me Fireball." Trying to remember what happened before I fell asleep, all I could recall was Kitzhaber, I mean Fireball, purring extraordinarily loud.

Sunday we went to visit my cousin Jewel all day, so I didn't have a chance to see if calling him Fireball would have any effect. On Monday, I called out, "Fireball" while he was in another room. As with most cats, he never reacted to being called, but this time he immediately ran in and jumped on my lap. Wife Sally asked about his name change and his strange behavior. Rather than sound crazy, I said that I was trying out "Fireball" because he was flaming orange, but had no idea why he ran to me.

Because I had always viewed cats as mystical and mysterious creatures, I was not as surprised by his behavior as you might expect. On Tuesday while Sally was out shopping, I called to Fireball. He came to my lap, again, and I am fairly sure I was awake when I heard what I think was him speaking to my brain; I guess you could call it telepathy, but I'm not sure. "I could tell when you called me Fireball that we had a link." As much as I was convinced that Fireball was speaking to me, I also wondered if I was crazy or having a stroke, but I 'heard' "No crazy, no stroke."

For a little while I thought about asking Fireball something only, I would know, before I realized how foolish that would be. Instead, I went along with the craziness and asked him a few questions.

"Why are you talking to me now?"

"From reading your mind, I could tell that we would be simpatico, and I was getting bored without any real conversation."

"Would you talk to Sally?"

"No, I can tell that she would want to tell everyone, but I think that you can keep this our secret. If you ever do think of telling anyone, imagine the reaction."

"Do cats commonly converse with people?"

"Not at all lately. Most cats can't talk. I'm special, as you should know. Of those that can talk, most are not interested. They either have nothing to say, or their human company is not worth talking to. A lot of people would kill talking cats. If you know your history, millions of cats that were the familiars of witches were killed. After that we rarely communicated with people."

"What do you think about being neutered?"

"Despite what humans may think of it, it really works for me. Whether I wanted to or not, if I was entire, I would be fighting the other toms to impregnate some local queen. Most likely, I'd get ripped up badly. Just like people who should know better, get drunk and drive anyway, we can't help ourselves as long as we have testosterone. Now I get all I want to eat, a clean dry place to sleep and avoid nasty jungle craziness."

"What's your thing with torturing your live prey?"

"What's your thing with war? OK, to answer your question, that is how we start the digestive process."

"Do cats have a theology?"

"Some, but not all cats, believe that we were created by a divine lion-like creature, which then made the other animals to keep us humble. We expect that on the day of truth all the other animals but cats and edible rodents will perish from the earth and paradise will be attained."

"I can't tell what you are thinking. Does your facial expression tell me anything?"

"You can't pivot your ears, and I can't do much with my face. If I'm hissing, stay away."

"Do related felines, like lynxes, have the ability to 'speak'?"

"No, we consider them to be retarded, but mostly the skill requires spending lots of time with humans."

"How do you feel about dogs?"

"When they don't want to kill me, I can take them or leave them. Some can be good companions and I know that a lot of people get all gooey over them. I have real reservations about their sanitary habits. The whole sniffing other dogs' butts and rolling in stinky things grosses me out."

"But you lick your own butt."

Fireball left the house without replying.

Over the next few weeks, Fireball and I continued to "converse", when Sally wasn't around to break our concentration. This was of course entertaining, but then I was laid off, and we had something bigger to be concerned about.

My problem then was how to monetize a telepathic cat. Fireball made it clear that he would not be involved in any silly show biz gig. If I tried, he would just clam up. I even tried to bribe him with a separate, well-furnished house of his own.

Since we are rich now, you probably wonder how I pulled it off. It turns out that Fireball is not the only smarty in the house. I told Sally, we needed to ignore our problems for a while and take a little vacation. My other cousin Shane, the rich investor, always liked Fireball and agreed to keep him while we went to Cannon Beach on the Coast.

After our vacation when we got Fireball back, I made a lot of successful investments. Fireball has his own small house now, but spends a lot of time with us. From time to time, he boards with Shane while we are out of town, so the money continues to roll in. I don't feel too bad about using Shane's expertise – he always treated Fireball better than he did us, and kept all of his investment ideas to himself. Sally is amazed at what an astute investor I've become.

Over the next several years, Fireball and I had a lot of philosophical conversations, talking about whatever came to mind. We learned to dance together. At first, we both tried dancing on our back legs, and then on all fours. Neither worked, so we each danced our own way. Sally was surprised because Fireball had never previously showed any sign of being interested in "tricks".

Of course, it couldn't last and it didn't. At a ripe old age Fireball had slowed down and even seemed to "talk" to me less. One day he came to me and said, "You are going to have to put me down. My time is growing short, and I don't want to suffer before I go. I have just one request. I want you to bury me under that tree in the backyard where all of the birds perch and torment me. All that screeching, knowing I can't get them. You know I'm unsure of the afterlife, but if I can, I want to haunt those bastards when I'm gone."

I didn't want to bother the birds, but I couldn't believe even a "talking" cat would become a ghost after death. Sally had been noticing that Fireball had declined a lot, so I wasn't surprised when she broached the subject of taking the last drive to the vet. After all of the love we had shared, we both shed some tears about losing our cat. Fireball surprised us again by dying before we could get him to the vet. That made it easy to grant his wish to be put to rest by the trunk of the tree.

After living with a telepathic cat, how could anything be impossible? Birds would land in the tree, but immediately fly away. Fantastic Fireball got his wish.

Published in *Dual Coast* and *Down In The Dirt*

Prime 4

JULIE COLLINS: We are back with our fourth interview with Dook, who represents the Angwins, or what we had called Yetis or abominable snowmen. Today, we'd like to talk about a controversial area, the beliefs or religion of the Angwin. Welcome back Dook.

DOOK: Same to you Julie.

JULIE COLLINS: So what is your religion or beliefs?

DOOK: We don't subscribe to anything which might be called a religion, but some of our mutant retrogrades have adopted some of the beliefs of the lands in which they live.

JULIE COLLINS: Some might think that you would be Buddhists given your proximity to Tibet.

DOOK: We have absolutely learned from our neighbors. Their emphasis on leading good lives in general resonates with us, and we learned yoga and meditation from them, but for practical rather than spiritual reasons. The idea of Nirvana does not appeal much to us. We like having a good time.

JULIE COLLINS: And what have you taken from the Hindus?

DOOK: Again, I would say their belief in ethical living, as is emphasized in most religions. The same is true of the lesser-known Zoroastrianism.

JULIE COLLINS: And their many gods and belief in reincarnation?

DOOK: First, I think that the emphasis on the multitude of "gods" is overdone. Secondly, we think that when we die, we are gone.

JULIE COLLINS: Islam?

DOOK: We do not disparage any belief as long as it does not condone violence. We have not had much contact with Muslims despite them living close by.

JULIE COLLINS: No eternal life, no supreme being?

DOOK: No. *Chuckles*. We don't imagine a giant bearded patriarch in the sky. The universe may be the ultimate intelligence, but there is no way that we would know.

JULIE COLLINS: What of Western Religions like Christianity, or smaller faiths like Latter Day Saints or Scientology?

DOOK: We have studied them and adapted anything that we find helpful. We like most of the teachings of Jesus, but suspect that he was misquoted on occasion.

JULIE COLLINS: So much for what you don't believe. What do you believe?

DOOK: As I mentioned, we simply believe in leading good lives. As isolated and few as we are, we must rely on mutual support. We have our mythology, parables and allegories which we don't necessarily take literally, but use as learning devices.

JULIE COLLINS: Could you give us some examples?

DOOK: Our legends say that early Angwin witnessed the extinct Harrapan civilization of the Indus River and learned ecological lessons from its demise. They cut down the forest and their land became desiccated. Lesson – don't destroy your home by overbuilding. It has been passed down that earlier lowland Angwin were there during the Vedic period of early Hinduism when the battles were fought and destruction was wrought. Lesson – avoid conflict. We wish that lesson was used more often, especially now in the Middle East.

There is Angwin folk wisdom. "I don't need any more snow or oxygen." "Try some condiments on your fungus." As you can imagine, these are particularly suitable for us.

JULIE COLLINS: Many religions, ethnic groups or nationalities believe that they have a founder. How about you?

DOOK: The elders tell a story about Angwine, a person of ambiguous sexuality who lived thousands of years ago in what was pre-civilization Iraq. He/she is supposed to resemble current Angwin and lived for hundreds of years with many husbands and wives in a rich kingdom. The story may be as real as Santa Claus, or it may be a concatenation of a number of real progenitors of the Angwin today.

JULIE COLLINS: I'm sure that I could ask a million more questions, or at least twenty, but that is all that I have prepared. Do you have any final comments?

DOOK: A couple. Our scholars ran across an account of a religion which died out, but in its early history it developed along with Judaism. Its beliefs speak to us more than other organized religions. Oddly, a description of it was published in the online journal *Potluck* – Elrod.

On a completely unrelated note, the major country that had spurned us recognizes us now that its leader has quit in disgrace.

Appeared in *Occulum*

Old

The Perfect Couple

Janet and Mike Wilkie were reading the morning newspaper at the breakfast table. Janet said, "Hey, we're the perfect couple or so says the newspaper."

Mike responded, "They finally got something right. I'm beautiful, and you're brilliant. Or, is it the other way around?"

"Clever Mike. They mention my painting and your business putting Oregon on the map. The reporter seems to think that both of us are beautiful and brilliant. Good thing they don't know that you're a secret junk food junkie, and I've got a gambling habit. Then there's our kids – Peg's secret abortion and Jason's marijuana indulgence."

The Fairy Tale Ends

Mike usually took the Jaguar to the office and Janet drove the huge Suburban to her clothes design shop. One day in December, Janet said half in jest, "Mike you have all of the fun. I want to take the Jaguar today." Fair minded Mike agreed that it was her turn to drive something sporty, so they traded.

As Janet was pulling away from a four way stop, a Ford beater ran the stop sign and hit the Jaguar on the passenger side. For the remainder of their lives, it would be an unspoken question: "Would she have been protected better in the Suburban."

After months in the hospital Janet was released in a wheelchair. The Wilkies were told that she would never walk again, but they hoped for a miracle.

While caring for Janet, Mike found out as much as he could about the driver of the beater that hit their Jag. The immediate salient facts were that Doug Jenkins was eighteen years old, had a record of misdemeanors, a very high alcohol blood level of .25% and tried to drive away after the accident. Mike was not satisfied with this surface account. Digging deeper, he found out that the driver was born to meth heads and had subsequently passed through a number of low rent foster homes. He was beaten in some and verbally abused in all of them. Even though he tested as very intelligent, he rarely passed his classes as he went from school to school.

After he felt he had all the information he needed, Mike discussed their course of action with Janet. Together they decided to urge the court for mercy when his case came up, and to support him after his sentence was passed. Mike and Janet were not religious, but they believed in second chances.

Adapting

Janet kept a couple of wheelchairs, one hand driven for short trips on level ground and an electric one for more complicated terrain. With the help of Mike's tech knowledge, the electric one had a phone, music, a GPS and several other technical doo-dads.

They indulged in whatever intimacy was available to them. They still enjoyed kissing and rubbing each other. Janet got particular pleasure out of back rubs and sometimes front rubs. Necessity became the mother of kink.

After their situation was somewhat stabilized, they had a serious talk. First, Mike asked Janet to give him her honest feelings.

"I hate that this has happened to me, but I'm not looking for the easy way out. It matters a lot to me that I have a loving husband and two beautiful children who are gathering around me rather than being turned off by my condition. Up until the accident, my life was a fairy tale. Maybe this is some kind of averaging, the sublime with the second rate. I still think that I have a lot to give. I'm trying to give hope to the disabled, I'm still working on my fashions, and the kids still ask me for advice. What I'd like to do now is see if I can work on fashions for the disabled, and I want to make sure that we can help the healing of the boy who hit me.

"Let me talk about you for a minute. You must never ruin your life because of me. You must never give up normal sex because I can't perform any more."

Mike said, "I didn't think that you would give up, but I wanted to hear you say it. I'm 100% in favor of your plan to be productive. I hope that you know that I will never stop loving you regardless of what happens. Mike never intended to cheat, but he wanted to make Janet happy.

All of this sounded fairly formal, but they both were relieved by the conversation.

Jason took over more responsibility at Gold, and Peg took a leave of absence.

Henry Charles had been the Chief Information Officer at Gold until he retired early with a pile of stock, convertible to several million dollars. He was an amateur sportsman and a playboy before he retired, and they became his fulltime pursuits when he retired. The paternity suit against him was an impediment to his plans until it was thrown out when his vasectomy was revealed. With no work to go to, he worked on his tennis game until he was winning senior tournaments.

They both had off-center views of life and truly egregious senses of humor. Their routine was for one to start off with a bad joke and the other one would try to "bottom" it.

Mike: "Why did dyslectic Fox Mulder of the X-files investigate the sad dental hygienist? Because she was a sighing flosser."

Henry: "Why is a sick raptor against the law? It's ill eagle."

Mike: "The beginner's book for ventriloquists is *Dummies For Dummies*."

Henry: "I give up. That is the worst."

They had talked off and on since the accident. When Henry thought Mike might be ready, he called Mike and said, "Why don't you visit with me at my cabin at Forchet and we do some fishing."

Forchet – pronounced *For-shay* – is a resort 25 miles up the Siletz River from the Oregon Coast. It is an expensive fishing camp, resort, and artist colony. Henry had the cabin for ten years.

Mike didn't think he could leave Janet, but when his family heard about the offer, they ganged up on him. Janet said, "What do you think, I'm some sort of invalid?" After a strained silence, she began to guffaw, followed by Jason and Peg and finally Mike. They continued to laugh and cry for five minutes. Jason and Peg knew how much he liked hanging out with Henry and how much he needed a break. He hadn't been out of the Portland area since the accident.

The next Monday, he loaded up the Subaru, which had replaced the Jaguar, with the fishing gear he hadn't used in a year and took off for Forchet. Within three hours he was greeted by Henry and ensconced in the cabin.

The next couple of days they did nothing but fish and make small talk. They had a lot to catch up on, but stayed away from "the accident". Mike had brought down some CDs of the electronic music he had been recording. Henry showed off his paintings, some of serene nature scenes from Oregon's beauty, and some of the wilder scenes of his girlfriends. They spent a little time on Portland's and Oregon's dysfunctional government, but that conversation had nowhere to go. Neither had any interest in shop talk.

Mike was surprised to notice that Henry looked several years older than the last time he had seen him. Henry noticed the stare and said, "Retirement is a lot of work. It's wearing me out."

Fishing was so poor that they were forced to take most of their meals at the local restaurant "Henri". Many had wondered about the French sounding names abounding at the resort. Very few knew the Finn that established the place had thought that French sounded classier than Finnish.

Mike wanted to know how many girlfriends Henry would have if he were poor.

"They all say that the money makes no difference."

"How many do you believe?"

"None."

They laughed. Henry was glad to see his old friend relaxing a little.

As Mike strolled around the town, he noticed that there were a lot older men with younger women, but they didn't all look like sugar daddies. It wasn't a big thing, but it was noticeable.

After a few days, Henry said ,"There's a better fishing spot a ways up the river, I'll show you the path if you are interested. It is several miles, so you may want to take your overnight gear. I've got to tell you, it could change your life."

Intrigued, Mike asked, "Change how?"

"You'll have to find out for yourself."

Challenged, Mike decided he had to go.

Rebecca

The next morning, Henry showed Mike to the path and said, "Keep going until the path hits the river."

It took almost all day to get to the fishing spot, but indeed the fishing was great. As he was about to set up his tent, he heard a feminine voice, "I don't see too many people this far up the river. What's your story?"

Mike turned around to answer, but paused before spoke. What he saw was a statuesque brunette with a Barbie figure. She was wearing a tank top and cutoffs. Her forehead came up to his nose. He imagined her in a beer commercial dressed in a bikini and f___ me pumps playing volleyball. After his mind returned, he told her, "Just a business man from Portland doing some fishing. What are YOU doing up here?"

"A long time ago, I decided to live off the grid. I built a little cabin out here and do some art carvings, which I trade for what little I need in Forchet. It is a simple life, but I like it."

"That sounds like a dream for some, but I couldn't handle it. I need my family and friends to keep me sane."

"Tell me about your family."

"Well, my wife Janet is an artist like you except that she paints and designs clothes. Son Jason works at my electronics business and daughter Peg is seriously trying to save the world with the "Whole World Blind' organization."

"I've heard about the 'Whole World Blind Foundation'. Now that we are old friends, maybe we should exchange names. I'm Rebecca."

"I'm Mike."

"Say Mike, I know that you were about to set up your tent, but I've got a second bed in my cabin that I think would be comfy, and I think that it might rain tonight."

"You're not worried about being attacked in the middle of night?"

"First, you don't know what weapons I've got and second, maybe you should be worried."

"I think neither of us should worry. I've never cheated, and never will. Now that that is cleared up I'll just cast my worries to the wind, which by the way, seems to be picking up."

It was just a short walk, and they were at the very modest cabin. Mike tested the mattress, and it was firm just the way he liked it. There were a variety of pillows for his comfort. After some small talk, he starting rereading some classic P.D. James that he had read a few years ago, and she worked on a small carving of a cedar tree. Soon, they said their good nights and went to their respective beds.

During the night Mike dreamed that Rebecca entered his bed and grabbed him. After a bit, dream Mike said, "I can't do this."

Rebecca responded, "You are not cheating, this is a dream." Her words turned loose his pent-up passion. After some missionary sex, his dream got kinkier and kinkier.

The next morning, Mike noticed his crotch was sticky. Later when he went outdoors to urinate – no indoor facilities – he was spraying in five directions. He thought, "This is the kinkiest wet dream I've ever had." Without giving any details, he mentioned to Rebecca that he had dreamed about her.

"A lot of men have," she replied. Mike had no problem believing it.

After a breakfast of venison, he bid Rebecca a fond farewell and smiled all the way back to Forchet. He noticed that he was very tired. Could dream sex wear him out that much?

Back at the cabin Henry said, "You look worn out. Tough walk?"

Mike didn't want to talk about Rebecca, so he just agreed, "Yup, I must be getting older."

Henry smirked knowingly and asked, "How was the fishing?"

"You were right, the fishing was good, and I brought some back, since you can't seem to catch anything."

Mike had planned a couple more days at Forchet, but the next day he got a call from Peg saying, "Mom's got an infection and has been hospitalized. Get home now."

At the hospital Janet said, "Don't worry, it is no big deal, I'll be out tomorrow. In case you think that I missed you, you haven't noticed all the young, good-looking doctors around here."

At 2.00 that morning Mike was called by the hospital and told, "We are sorry to tell your wife passed away an hour ago."

"I can't believe it; she was scheduled to be released this morning."

"Sir, come in at 8.00 and we will give you a full explanation. Again, you have our deepest sympathy."

Mike called Jason and Peg, had a few drinks and watched bad late-night TV. There was no chance that he would get to sleep. At the hospital, they got another shock. The doctor explained, "Ms. Wilkie's death had little to do with her accident or her infection. While those events may have hastened her death, we have discovered a congenital heart defect that could have caused her death at any time. If it is any consolation, she far outlived her life expectancy. I can only hope that this information makes her passing a little easier to accept."

In a daze, Mike went home and broke the news to Joseph and Sue. Mike had been close to his in-laws and they all tried to do what they could to support each other. Joseph and Sue had known about the heart defect and were not as surprised as Mike expected.

"We learned of it when Janet was an infant, but because there was no treatment, we decided not to tell her for fear that it would worry her about something which could not be helped. In spite of our loss, we feel good about what she did with her life in the time that she had. We never told you because we thought that you would spend your life worrying about her."

Mike had been feeling draggy even before the accident.

His doctor confirmed that he was only about five years younger than his chronological age as opposed to the excellent ten years younger that he had been. Everyone put it down to the strain and stress.

Life As A Widower

For a month or so Mike acted like a zombie, stumbling around, talking in monosyllables. All the while his children and friends, while also suffering, were advising him to work on ways of easing the pain.

He had to agree, so he finally listened to their advice – get involved in work, socialize, and try to find things to laugh about.

When he went back to work, he found that Jason had taken over in his absence. His executives pretended interest in his ideas, but were following Jason's lead. After a few days of being righteously pissed, he realized that this was what he was working towards even before Janet's accident and he was really proud of his son. He wondered, *What can I do with my daughter? Maybe I should be improving the world, rather than finding more ways that people can isolate themselves with their electronic gizmos.* He remembered that one of his wild ideas was generating energy with tidal power. Peg had been telling him that the world needed more drinkable water and power. Tidal machines could make the power, which in turn could be used for desalinization.

He spent a few weeks with Peg talking about the best places for making tidal power sources. He took a few million of his own money and started crowd funding for the project. He knew that practical tidal power was at least a decade out, so he found the brightest young engineers he could and some political operators. He knew that he had more than an engineering problem; he also had a public relations problem. People were wedded to the new lower prices of petrol, and getting them to change wouldn't be easy.

Eventually, after a quick assessment, he had to admit to himself that he was a very marketable male. It is hard to top rich, tall and good looking even though his long marriage had dulled his dating skills. In spite of that he found no trouble finding dates at the various charitable events that he attended. He was amazed by the variety of responses that he got. Some wanted no physical contact at all, but expected to be taken to the most expensive restaurants. He didn't wonder why they were single. Others expected sex immediately. After months of celibacy, he felt a little guilty about how easy he was. Not too guilty.

After a few weeks of this, he had a date with Jill Epstein, a fascinating woman. On the first date she told him what she called a "Jewish Joke".

"A middle-aged woman is sitting in a beach chair on Miami Beach. A hunky very pale guy sits down beside her. She asks why he is so muscular and pale. He says, 'I spent ten years working out inside a prison cell for killing my wife.' She says, 'So you're single.' "

Jill explains, "Here is the point. Look, you are a very eligible bachelor. You've got to expect to be hit on by women regularly. *Let me tell you about my situation.* I've made a lot of money getting divorced. Husband one was playing around and was happy to give me a big settlement to save his reputation. Pretty much the same thing with husband two but in his case, he was playing with boys. Bigger settlement. *At this point* I'm pretty much done with marriage, but I like sex. A lot. And I like variety. I suggest that we start an open relationship. I think that we could be good for each other. We are both intelligent people, so if the sex ever gets boring, we can talk. Both of us could see other people."

This sounded good to Mike, so they started at his house that evening and Jill delivered on all of her promises.

Mike's recovery from his loss was not that unusual except in one sense. Every night since Janet died, he had lucid dreams of Rebecca. None of them were particularly erotic. They could be eating, talking or taking a hike. The inexplicable part of the dreams was that Rebecca would talk about things that Mike didn't know. She told him about the book *Wild* which Mike knew nothing about. After waking up, he checked on what he had learned in the dream and found out that it matched the book exactly. Mike was at a loss to explain how that could happen.

Back To Forchet

One morning Mike woke up and said out loud. "I want to see Henry and Rebecca again. I'm going back to Forchet." After checking with Henry, he cancelled all of his plans for the next month and took off.

When he met Henry, he asked without any preamble, "What do you know about Rebecca?"

"After you talk to her, I'll tell you what I know."

Rebecca wasn't in town; they supposed she must be back at her cabin.

Mike started early the next day so he would have time in the afternoon to get her story. Before they spoke Mike noticed that Rebecca looked a few years older than the last time he had seen her. She had a few gray hairs this time. After a few preliminaries at her cabin, Rebecca said, "Please listen to my story without interrupting. You will want to interrupt me, but please listen to the whole story before saying anything."

"My mother was a Siletz Indian. I'm the result of a one-night stand with a disgraced Oregon politician. You would recognize his name. At least he sent enough money to my mother to keep her in comfort in return for her silence. We had enough money for me to get a good education at the U of O. After I got back from college my mother asked me, 'How old do you think I am?' I'd never really thought about it before, but people mistook us for sisters. She said she was forty even though she looked like twenty-five. She then said, 'I'm going to tell you a secret that you won't believe. I used a ritual that a very few Siletz women have used. In earlier times most avoided the deep woods because they believed that is where evil spirits dwell, and in more recent years the ritual was largely forgotten. First, I made my way to the headwaters of the Siletz and bathed in the waters and then said, 'Give me life.' According to the ritual I had to lie with men after telling them that I was taking part of their life. Since then, I have not aged. I was willing to abase myself and they were willing to surrender a portion of their lives in order to partake of my perfect body.' Of course, I didn't believe her, but she seemed much younger than her years."

"I got a job in Portland and visited her from time to time. I forgot about her ridiculous folk tale. With your recent loss of Janet, it may be painful to hear, but a year after I heard her story, she died after being hit by a hit and run driver. I came back to clear out her house. After a few days in Forchet, I realized how much I hated the city and wanted to return to the Siletz. With my small inheritance I built the cabin where I live now. As a lark, I hiked the short distance to the headwaters of the Siletz and completed the ritual. While at the lodge one night, I was picked up by a handsome tourist and I told him the deal. You may think me immodest, but I truly believe that I can deliver the ultimate pleasure. He didn't believe the part about losing some of his life so he was ever so eager to lie with me. The next day, despite some twinges of guilt, I felt great physically. He felt a little run down, despite reveling in our evening together."

"After that I would take on men as needed. Sometimes I enjoyed it, but mostly I felt degraded. There were married men, ugly men, short men, stupid men and mean men, but I stayed young and they got old. Do you think that I look forty?"

"After many years, I could not go on. Aging had to be better than the life I was leading. This was about the time that you showed up. You don't know it, but I recognized you immediately from pictures and stories in the Oregonian and Portland Magazine. I was amazed that after years in the news, no one had found anything negative about you. Most of the men I have known would have played on my sympathy about your wheelchair bound wife. Instead, you declared your monogamy. At that point, I decided I would break the spell, whatever the cost. It didn't hurt your cause that you were easy on the eyes. Your dream about me the night that you stayed with me was not a dream, but a little bit of magic. I was right that sleeping with you without telling you the bargain broke the spell, but what I didn't know is that it would take years from both of us. I can't apologize enough to you for what I did."

"That's the story. Your turn."

"I can't believe it"

"Would it help you to believe if I told you the acts of love that you remember from your dream in my cabin or if I told you about the dreams, you have back in Portland? Even though the original spell is broken, I still have some magic."

"Now I can't believe it and I can't disbelieve it."

"Can you forgive me for the wrong that I have done you?"

"Love conquers all and you may not believe ME now, but I do love you."

Before leaving Forchet, Mike asked Henry if he had accepted Rebecca's bargain.

"Yes, several times."

"You were willing to give up years of your life?"

"I wanted to keep at her until she admitted I was her best."

"Did she?"

"As far as you know. Seriously, as much as I liked her, I knew that she would never settle for me, and I couldn't stand to lose any more years."

Mike was sorely irritated with Henry until he remembered that without Henry, he never would have met Rebecca.

Ten Years After Plus A Few Months

Mike and Rebecca have aged normally. They are celebrating their tenth anniversary. Mike's friends and family love Rebecca. His guy friends think that he is a lucky dog. The women envy Rebecca.

Mike toasts first, "No one has been as fortunate in love as I."

Rebecca takes her turn to toast and angrily says, "Living with Mike has cost me my youth." The guests squirm uneasily. Then she smiles broadly and finishes, "But I wouldn't trade it for anything."

Fly

Locals from Igaluit on Baffin Island north of mainland Canada found what appeared to be odd pebbles which were exposed when the recent heat wave melted a layer of snow. As the sun warmed the "pebbles", their shells broke and flying insects flew out. The first poor unfortunates who examined the insects were stung and died from the multiple venomous stings. The terrified survivors barricaded themselves in their houses.

The biologists and exterminators from the mainland were quickly overwhelmed. Nothing in the exterminators' toolkit had any effect on the insects, and the mainlanders that didn't die were quickly run off.

Out of any other options, the remaining human population of Baffin was evacuated to mainland Canada. With only 6,532 survivors from the original 11,000 human inhabitants, the resettlement was not too difficult.

During and after the resettlement, flyovers revealed the bones of polar bears, foxes, rabbits, caribou and wolves picked clean. Because Baffin didn't amount to much, the invasion of the insects was just viewed as a small problem of global warming. It was assumed that the insects, now called Death Flies, would die out with nothing left to eat, or that they would form cysts again and become inactive.

Professor Emil Yancy from the University of Laval in Montreal assured the public that the flies were adapted to cold temperatures and would not venture south. A month later, the flies had invaded Hall Beach in northern Nunavut on the Canadian mainland. Yancy and his colleagues backtracked quickly, suggesting that the flies were reproducing extremely fast and mutating like a virus, adapting to warmer weather. They were no longer consulted.

Siberia then reported its first Death Flies. The governments of the world became serious and seriously scared about the threat of human extermination. Homes could be sealed, but no one could leave and a truly safe sealing kept out fresh air and ended in the occupants' asphyxiation.

The capriciousness of the miles wide cloud of death flies made the invasion even more frightening. The horde skipped Edmonton, but hit Calgary in Alberta.

All radio and television was preempted by the film of the plague taken by helicopters. The world was told that the only poisons strong enough to kill the flies would kill even more people than the flies would.

On October 31, a few days after Calgary was deserted, the retired couple Duke and Sally, in Lake Oswego, Oregon, discussed the situation. Sally said, "We gotta get out of here. Go as far south as we can. Our lives are at stake. Just leave everything and save our lives."

Duke, who like a former president was always certain, but frequently wrong, said, "There is nothing to worry about. They aren't in the US and they will never get here. I've got that from an unimpeachable source. The best thing that we can do is turn off the TV. All it does is depress us and none of our shows are on."

Partly because she had deferred to Duke through many years of marriage and partly because he was so convinced, Sally decided to accept his word that they would be safe.

At 6pm Duke looked out the window and saw his neighbor, who was his best friend and tennis partner, running around his yard. Duke said, "I see Jim is wearing a black Ninja outfit for Halloween and practicing some martial arts routine... ooooh shoot!" At that point Jim collapsed on the ground, twitched and died. Duke saw that the sky was black and heard the buzzing roar grow louder.

Tears rolled down Duke's face and he said, "How could I ever have listened to that crackpot evangelist Samuel Sanctum. He said, 'The US is special. God would never allow the plague in our holy land.' I've been such a fool for so many years. I'm so sorry. Get the gun."

"The gun won't stop the flies."

"The gun isn't for the flies, it's for us."

Sally thought, *Heck, I'm going to die soon, but at least I lived to hear Duke admit he's wrong.*

Published in *Commuter Lit, Yellow Mama* and the defunct *Nugget Tales*

Prime 5

JULIE COLLINS: I'm very pleased to be able to have another interview with Dook, a representative of our closest relatives, what we call the yetis and what they call the Angwin.

We have talked about some Angwin basics and your successful attempt to create homeland. Today I'd like to talk about your daily life. We've already learned about your sustainable life, and your creative romantic life. Would you tell us what a normal day is like for you folk?

DOOK: Glad to. We always try to get a good night's sleep and then work on our homes and communal structures and harvest our food. None of those activities take very long, so we have plenty of time for entertaining ourselves.

JULIE COLLINS: I'm sure that our in-house audience and those listening and viewing at home would like the details filled in.

DOOK: Let me start on what you might call our infrastructure. Most of us live under the snow and we have tunnels connecting our homes. Depending on the weather, we may have to create troughs and pits for water runoff or repair damaged tunnels. At least we never want for building materials – snow and ice.

Chuckles.

JULIE COLLINS: If I may break in here, are all homes connected to all other homes?

DOOK: Oh no, the number of connecting tunnels would be astronomical. Want me to do some illustrative mathematics for you?

JULIE COLLINS: Oh, please no! But I do wonder how many houses you have and how many live in a house?

DOOK: I don't know the answer to the first question and if

I did, I would not want the answer known. As indicated in an earlier interview, we do have enemies, and we would like to keep some secrets. As to your second question, anywhere from one to fifty may live in a single home.

JULIE COLLINS: Fifty? Are extended families common amongst Angwin?

DOOK: Our social structures are more varied than among humans. In some cases there may be several generations in one house. In another, it may resemble a sorority or a fraternity. Also, polyamory is widely practiced with various mixtures of genders. Less sensational is the most common arrangement, mother, father and 2.5 children. The 2.5 is a joke unless it isn't funny.

JULIE COLLINS: Is homosexuality common?

DOOK: About the same as with humans, also roughly the same percent as left handers.

JULIE COLLINS: How about you personally?

DOOK: I'd like to keep my private life private out of consideration for my family.

JULIE COLLINS: You mentioned in an earlier interview that you are relatively impervious to the cold. Are your homes warm enough naturally, or are they heated somehow?

DOOK: We don't need anything beyond the heat generated by living in close quarters, but we like hot baths and we get into the sunshine when available.

JULIE COLLINS: How do you heat water?

DOOK: We have become very good with solar energy. Our retrogrades have been very helpful.

JULIE COLLINS: Remind us about the retrogrades.

DOOK: We produce some mutant children occasionally who look like humans, but are as smart as we are.

JULIE COLLINS: You mentioned time for entertainment.

DOOK: We have games and quizzes. Some of the Angwin are excellent sculptors. We use both stone and snow. The snow is used as an impermanent medium, something like the sand in Japanese gardens.

Over the years, the retrogrades have furnished us with up-to-date technology for writing and film. As a result, we have quite a library of indigenous literature and film, plus some of the best human product.

JULIE COLLINS: You mentioned earlier that you have a stable population because your women can time their births. How is that done?

DOOK: I believe that I mentioned before that we have developed various kinds of fungi. One increases a woman's fertility and another one shuts it down.

If I may interject an interesting sidelight, a part of what we offered to the rest of the world in return for our homeland, was information about our discoveries. The birth preventing fungi is very popular among women in countries controlled by patriarchal societies and fundamentalist religions. The male rulers feel that power comes from an out-of-control population of the poor and uneducated, but the women have found access to contraband fungi and are taking control of their births. I'm sure that those brave women can improve the fortunes of their countries.

JULIE COLLINS: That is indeed good news. My final question is related to your last answer. You mentioned your fungi diet. What else do you eat?

DOOK: I mentioned our solar power earlier. We also grow a variety of vegetables with hydroponics. I brought some peppers with me this time. Take this basket.

JULIE COLLINS: Dook, thanks for taking the time again to talk with me. Any final thoughts?

DOOK: Thanks for all of the people and governments that

have supported us. We feel that humans and Angwin can have a beneficial relationship in the coming years.

Published in *Occulum*

Asteroid

Ray detection

The outer space probe Arrow detected an increase in cosmic rays traveling towards earth beyond the orbit of Pluto. The intensity of the rays increased by a factor of ten and then Arrow became silent. NASA made the report to the White House with the rather panic-inducing possibility that the rays could wipe out all life on earth. One sardonic joker in the inner circle said, "At least we don't have to worry about asteroids anymore." NASA hedged its bets by saying that the best case was an interruption in all electronics. After all, the incident was unprecedented, so no one could say with certainty what the results would be. Not that it helped, but they narrowed the cause down to two or three supernovae observed in historic times. Some true believers at the highest levels of government wondered if their death would be from the star of Bethlehem.

The leading edge of the rays was discovered at ten times the distance from Pluto. President Burton had no idea what to do. His skill set was campaigning, raising cash and pushing expensive bills without any way to pay for them. One thing that he did do well was pick men who were knowledgeable and skilled. As a result, he put Chief of Staff Duke Hanley in charge of liaison with NASA chief Sally Olsen. They got adjacent rooms in a DC hotel to keep people in government from wondering what was happening. Each took open leaves of absence.

Preparation

At their first meeting, Duke asked, "Level with me, how bad do you really think it is?"

"I think that it could be comparable to one of the great asteroid collisions with earth that caused mass extinctions like the one that killed the dinosaurs. Unlike an asteroid collision, the deaths won't happen immediately, plants and animals will die slowly. What cosmic rays do is mess with the DNA. Not only will there be a massive die off, there will be mutations, mostly fatal, some neutral, or even improvements. We've got eighty days to prepare."

"So what can we do about it?"

"The greatest effects will be on exposed life and that at the higher elevations. It wouldn't be practical to get lead suits for everyone or move them all into caves. Even if everyone stayed indoors, it wouldn't save the plants and animals we live on. Being indoors wouldn't be perfectly safe for people either."

"So far you have told me what we can't do about it."

"Are you religious?"

"No."

"Me neither, so praying is out. We can probably save some people from death by moving them into caves or fortified structures. Long term, after the rays have passed, the problem may be with finding suitable food for those that survive the initial barrage without getting cancer."

"It sounds like we may end up with some healthy people, a lot of ill people and not much future. How do we choose the people to save, what do we do about the ill people and how do we get to long term survival?"

"I can't answer the first part. As for the second part, it depends in part on how many we save. If most of the people die, there may be enough resources to go around, particularly if you like eating cockroaches. Seriously, if there are a lot fewer people, it may be easier to feed them with surviving plants and animals."

"OK, Sally, you've given me enough very scary information to try to build a plan around. I'm going to need to call a lot of people tonight, so let's call it a wrap. Do you want to meet in your room tomorrow or back in my room?"

"Your room is fine."

At the next meeting, Duke summarized his plan. "We hold a worldwide asteroid preparedness drill. The leaders that we can trust will be apprised of the game, others will get the cover story. We will explain that buildings and caves will be used to protect people from the effects of a possible asteroid impact in the next year. We'll make a survey of buildings which offer the best protection and find the best routes for getting to those buildings. The caves will be reserved for personnel deemed necessary for humanity's survival. Under the cover of the 'drill', we'll provision those caves as best we can. My idea is to accept that millions, if not billions will die, but I can't see anything better. Informing the world that we're going to be hit by massive cosmic rays is folly in my mind. Clearly, this is the Cliff Notes version. What do you think? I'd love for you to tell me it's a crackpot idea and you've got something much better."

"Could you get me a drink while I think about it? How about some scotch?"

"Coming up."

Sally drank about half of her drink and said, "I think that what you are trying to do is to get prepared while keeping the real reason secret to avoid panic. Is that right?"

"Yes."

"I agree that your goal is sensible and your approach reasonable. I'm afraid that I don't have a better idea. My guess is that you need to work on the details and I need to talk to my people at NASA."

The next day while Sally was talking to NASA, Duke ran his plan past the President. Burton said, "Fine work. First rate. You go ahead and handle all of the details." Burton's response was just what Duke expected, since the President always had others do the heavy lifting.

Duke then made calls to three cabinet secretaries to prepare them for the job ahead – Jackson at Defense, Williams at State and Gomez at Interior. Jackson would organize the logistics of moving people into safer areas and obtaining food and whatever would be needed for a lengthy stay in shelters, Williams would contact the leaders of other countries with either the true story or the cover story and Gomez would inventory shelters and caves around the country.

At that point Duke noticed he had never asked how long it would take the cosmic rays to pass. It seems that somehow, he had been distracted, probably by Sally. He immediately called Sally to get the answer. When he asked, she was equally dumbfounded that he had never asked and she hadn't volunteered the information. Maybe she was distracted too. "Crap, Duke, we have to get our heads straight. The rays will pass in a month after they start."

Over the next month they jointly kept up with the preparations. As expected, a lot of people doubted the cover story, but oddly no one guessed at the truth. Both the left and the right wings kept coming up with conspiracy theories claiming that the real reason for the exercises was to enslave the public.

The thoroughly ignorant wondered why the government wasn't doing something to destroy errant asteroids as was done in the movies *Deep Impact* and *Armageddon*. Exasperated, but patient government official had to keep repeating why the methods portrayed in those movies wouldn't work in real life.

While the physical work was being done stockpiling medicine and food, and preparing hardened sites for protecting important people, the VIP committee consisting of Duke, Sally and the cabinet secretaries Jackson, Williams and Gomez concentrated on the list of the necessary survivors. Farmers, engineers from all disciplines, physicists, chemists, medical personnel and mathematicians were at the top of the list.

The first draft was disproportionately Asian and Jewish given their prominence in the sciences and medicines. Everybody, including the female members Olsen and Williams, insisted on more females. If the cosmic catastrophe was bad enough to kill all of those that weren't completely protected against the rays, women would be more important to repopulate the world than males. Jackson complained about blacks being shortchanged and Gomez argued for more Latinos. After much haranguing and consulting data bases, the essential list was completed along with alternates for those on the list that wouldn't go to the shelters or were otherwise unavailable. The rest of the available safe spaces were filled by a random selection of those deemed young, healthy and multi-talented.

Aftermath

In most cities there was enough capacity in fairly well shielded buildings to shelter the urban population, but many people were not convinced to go to them. Many stayed home and many were outdoors when the cosmic rays hit earth. Previously appointed wardens moved as many as possible into some kind of shelter. When nothing else worked, the cosmic ray warning was used. There were so many skeptics, that the second-class shelters weren't filled.

In most developed countries the majority of the population had some kind of shelter for the month of cosmic ray bombardment. Less developed countries were less lucky.

Assessment

For several months after the rays passed through there were no obvious health problems. Electronics recovered nicely.

The major reaction was relief, but George Hughes, a celebrity trial lawyer, filed a class action suit against just about everyone involved in the planning. All of those involved in the planning had been indemnified against damages by executive order, so the suit was filed against the Federal Government. After both sides had their say, the Supreme Court threw out the suit, claiming that it did not have jurisdiction. Over a hundred websites were developed to claim that there was no increase in cosmic rays despite every reliable scientist acknowledging the major increase in rays.

After consulting with Hanley and Olsen, Burton gave a speech starting with, "Yes we may have over-prepared, but would you have wanted us to under-prepare?" and went on to praise the work of the cosmic ray team.

Sally told Duke, "Better than I predicted, worse than I hoped."

Julie Lanson, the secretary of Health and Human Services, decreed that a sample of those who had the most exposure to the rays should be medically examined. Of the three thousand that were examined, 20% were found to have cancer and all had changes to their DNA. From those statistics, she projected an extra 2.6 million would have cancer in the US alone. The increase in cancer shut up most of those that claimed there had never been excess cosmic rays, but created a health crisis all around the world. For countries without much health care, the richer nations sent tons of pain killers because the richer nations had their hands full with their own health care.

Lanson instituted a triage approach to the cancer crisis. Those that had a good chance of a cure would get normal treatment. People with a possibility of recovery were put on a waiting list and those who were terminal were placed in hospice treatment. Given the huge influx of those to hospice treatment, a crash program to train hospice staff was initiated.

Not only humans had health problems. 27% of mammals that lived above ground died within three months of the bombardment, according to Under Secretary of Agriculture Jay Simmons. Other forms of animals either were underground or underwater, protected by scales or feathers or simply more resilient like the infamous cockroaches.

The effect on plant life was, in a word, "bizarre". Some plants such as squash and cauliflower died out completely. The "supertasters" that could not stand the smell and taste of certain healthy foods were pleased, until they heard that seeds for all of the dead species were held in the Svalbard Global Seed Vault and had not been harmed at all by the cosmic rays. Some tomatoes grew so large that their stems could not support them. An apple variety grew as large as cantaloupes. A few poisonous plants were no longer poisonous, and some that had not been were now. All animals and humans had to adjust to a moving target as to what was edible and what wasn't.

The initial media reaction was to proclaim that this was the worst disaster ever to hit the planet. The reputable fact checkers "Reality Inc" immediately started to research the claim and ended up classifying what came to be known as "The Bombardment" as only number seven on the all-time worst list after some plagues, wars and influenza epidemics.

Bad Politics 1

The size of the catastrophe was enough to get the owner of the huge Lucky Penney casino in Las Vegas, Jason Atkins, to start another political party, Revolution. Atkins claimed that he would have handled the crisis much better than Burton, not knowing that Burton adhered to his hands off policy during the crisis. Atkins said he would have built underground caverns large enough to hold the whole US population. Despite the impossibility of his idea, he got a large following from the ignorant and the paranoid and he threatened to run against Burton in the next election.

As Atkins' following grew, President Burton called in Hanley and Olsen. "Let's be honest. I'm not too bright, but I've got a way with people. People love me from the time that I played "The Benevolent Billionaire" on TV ten years ago. As long as things are going well, I have my staff and cabinet officers handle things, and I get the credit. Everybody wins. I was fortunate to come into office when we were at peace and the economy was cruising along. The bombardment made it clear how useless I am and I don't want to sink to the level of that Atkins moron just to stay in office. My one great talent is evaluating people. Both of you are qualified to be president. If one of you is willing, I'll appoint you Vice President and then resign. Don't worry about Jenkins; he's tired of his do-nothing job and wants to return to his family and start the Jenkins Foundation. Feel free to consult with him, but nobody else. Why don't you two talk it over and get back to me tomorrow."

Later, Sally started off with, "I just want to go back to NASA. You'd be great as president and please don't think that I'm doing this for you. A scientist has never been a president for good reason. The people want someone who is a leader, not a thinker. Oops, I didn't mean that as insult. I mean someone who is not JUST a thinker."

"If I do this, I could appoint you to some office befitting your talents."

"Nope, when our relationship becomes public, you'd be charged with nepotism." They had become engaged during The Bombardment when they realized that they wanted to spend their lives together following their many previous romantic misadventures. Duke had made the mistake of marrying a woman that turned out to be a lesbian and Sally's success had led to her intimidating almost all men.

"I guess that some military men have made good presidents and some haven't. Nobody has done it since Eisenhower."

"Plus, I couldn't be the first woman president."

The call to the vice president affirmed that Jenkins was fully behind Burton's plan.

The shuffle went smoothly. With Hanley as president, Atkins' appeal was blunted without having Burton as a target. Atkins was not smart enough to find out that Hanley was a major force behind the preparation for The Bombardment.

Bad Politics 2

With the myriad problems with the health of people, animals and plants, the Federal and State welfare bills increased by 50%. The discontent from the poor led to the "Eat The Rich" movement, which everyone assumed was metaphorical. Sandy Bernard's plan was to expropriate any business making more than a million dollars annually and run it by the government. As the new movement gained millions of followers, Duke became frightened about the total collapse of the country if Bernard prevailed. In desperation, he convened the titans of industry and the idle rich. He gave them an alternative: "You stick with me and we double your taxes and you donate half your liquid assets to charity, and you get to keep the rest. Try to block me on this and you get Bernard. Which is it?" Enough of them stuck with Duke to mitigate Bernard's appeal.

After thirteen months with no new threats and with the recovery going well, Duke got a call from Gomez saying, "Super humans have taken over Eastern New Mexico."

The Evolution Of Bill Bane

It started with the announcement that there would be a worldwide drill to prepare for a possible asteroid impact in the next year. At the time, I assumed that it was more government lies. I didn't trust anything that I heard coming out of politicians or the lamestream press.

My wife had divorced me years ago because of my continuous anger and fights, both verbal and physical. All I could get were menial jobs because I was a dropout with a drinking problem. I lived in a cheap one-bedroom apartment in the Parkrose area of Portland, Oregon. The name on the door was Bill Bane. Bane was the name of the game for our family of losers.

Naturally I bucked all of the government rules during the active part of the drill. I wandered the streets and broke into the houses and businesses of those I considered fools for seeking better shelter. To further show my defiance, I ran up and down Sandy, the main drag through town, nearly naked.

At the end of the drill, President Burton, the lying bastard, admitted it was all a ruse to cover up for something else – a cosmic ray bombardment. He must have thought we'd believe a second lie. He even found a bunch of science toadies, the same scamsters that tried to sell global warming, to back him up.

Oddly, things started happening which made me start to question my skepticism. I began to read books, which I had never done before. In fact, the reason that I quit school was that I hated reading, and didn't understand a lot of words. After The Bombardment, as it was known, I read with comprehension. A book on cosmic rays made perfect sense to me and before that gravity had been a mystery. Rather than my usual breakfast, lunch and dinner of burgers, fries and cokes, while watching TV, I started a vegan diet and exercising. In a few weeks, I had lost thirty pounds and was running ten miles a day.

The change in my relationships was less quantifiable, but just as real. As I became friendlier and more generous to those around me, they were kinder to me. With my new attitude, and svelte body, I noticed babes eyeing me. Previously I only got lucky with lushes at closing time.

At this point, my drinking was confined to a healthy glass of red wine with dinner. I had moved on from being a counter worker at Burger Biggy to become a beginning ad writer at the international firm Sheridan & Philomath. With my new charm and intelligence, I was hired on the spot despite my abysmal work record and education, and could afford the best food and drink. For nostalgia, I went to my old watering hole, "Inn Between". I saw most of the usual barflies, except for Jodi Mitchell, the drunk in residence. I asked Shep, the owner and bartender, what happened to her.

Jodi Too

"Weirdest thing, she started talking funny, like a high school graduate, drank less and less and then just disappeared. None of my rummies have seen her for days."

I had a glass of the best red that they had, "Bleeding Gums", and left for the last time.

Even before I saw her again, I concluded that she had the same kind of transformation that I had. When I did see her, it was at our library, the kind of place that neither one of us had ever been before. I literally bumped into her coming around a shelf in the astronomy section. As I picked her up, we simultaneously said, "Cosmic Rays". I'm not sure how I recognized Jodi – she had lost thirty pounds since the last time I had seen her and her skin was no longer jaundiced, but had become a healthy pink.

Later over a smoothie, we compared notes. She said, "I started exercising and stopped drinking. I've been working on anything from the library and Wikipedia that is of interest. I understand multivariate calculus now, but failed algebra before I dropped out of school. Now I eat lots of fruits and vegetables and no red meat. My mind and body have completely transformed since The Bombardment. The only thing that makes sense is that instead of being unaffected like the majority or sickened like millions, our DNA has been improved."

I told her, "Pretty much the same story for me. How about we study together to absorb anything that will be useful or of interest to us?"

"Sounds good. Let's start tonight. What sounds like fun, eastern thought, or organic chemistry?"

"Let's start with eastern thought and then alternate between science and culture."

"Let's make it a three cycle rotating with physical skills as a third option."

"I like it."

We continued like that for weeks. The most pleasant study was tantric yoga. Although we had several drunken hook-ups in our prior existence, they were nothing like our new physical / spiritual relationship. We learned that we had become yogistes and Buddhists by independent discovery.

We concluded, accurately, if the two of us had evolved, there must be others. We read stories in the news about the town drunk in Dodge, Kansas becoming mayor after turning her life around completely in a short period of time. A mediocre sprinter at the University of Oregon recently set the world record in the 100 meters with the phenomenal time of 9.5 seconds. So far, the public was curious, but the number of articles was fairly small. We correctly assumed that many of the evolved didn't want to go public out of fear of the reaction to their status.

Evolved organized

Jodi got the idea of forming a "club" of the evolved. In order to do that, we put blind items in major newspapers reading "Feeling Better, Doing Better? Tell your story to PO Box 5820 Portland, OR 97218." We got responses about broken marriages being healed, weightlifting records being set, solutions to previously insoluble math problems and other stories of improvement. Most of those that wrote to us had improved intelligence and were smart enough to know how it had happened. In order to stay in touch with what turned out to be thousands of the evolved, we set up a "dark" website "Better", but in this case not one to abuse children or sell drugs, but to find out more about the phenomenon.

While we were working on that, I decided to find out what was going on in my body. That was one of the few things that I couldn't determine on my own. A trusted doctor checked me out thoroughly and found several anomalies:

- I had an increased frontal cortex compared to the norm, the "human" part of the brain, which made me smarter;
- My brain stem, the "reptile" part of the brain, was reduced from the normal, which reduced my animal behavior such as territoriality;
- My muscles were becoming stronger like a chimpanzee's;
- Also chimpanzee-like I had become hairier, something I had not previously noticed with all of the other miraculous changes; and
- There were other changes to my organs which were unexplained improvements.

85

Jodi then checked in at the same doctor and found similar improvements.

From the various responses we got from our survey on the dark site "Better", we found that some of our respondents had similar results from their doctors.

Most of the evolved had kept their heads down, but a few were doing incredible things in public, too many to recount. The five-foot-tall white boy that could dunk two handed and blocked LeBron James; the five-year-old that accurately corrected his first-grade teacher on many occasions and the forty-year-old woman that high jumped more than two meters. It was too much to keep secret. Social media started it and newspapers began to catch up. A few people came up with the truth, but there were more with conspiracy theories – mad scientists or a government project to produce super soldiers.

New Mexico

After checking the twitter feeds and reading some newspapers, Jodi said, "New Mexico." I immediately knew what she meant and agreed. We'd have to raise a lot of money, but we could start a colony in Eastern New Mexico. I thought of Mike Wilkie.

Mike was a good friend from working with him on an ad for Gold, his huge software company. He was a very happy guy who had the phenomenal fortune to marry a second terrific woman a few years after the death of his first wife. With his big local company that had, unlike most others started in Oregon, stayed local and his beneficent civic engagement, he was the most popular man in town. Because the "new" Bill could match him in intelligence and sophistication, we had bonded immediately.

He was not at all surprised when I told him my plan to start a colony of the evolved in Eastern New Mexico. He had already divined what was going on with the new and improved humans. "Great idea Bill. Eastern New Mexico is known for being the safest place in the US and still has low land prices. I think that I can stake you to enough money to get started."

"What can I do for you, Mike?"

"I wouldn't worry about that right now. Maybe Gold can be the software of your evolved geniuses."

When I told Jodi, she said, "You can't have all of the fun Bill. I'm going to get on "Better" and see who wants to join us and work on the easements and purchases that we will need."

As we worked on that with as much stealth as possible, the word was starting to leak out – "Super Men And Women Among Us" read an Oregonian headline. As always, a lot of the reporting was wrong. There were reports of invisible people, people that could lift Cadillacs (in reality, nothing larger than a Mini) and walk through walls. The reports got exaggerated to the point of suggesting that some of us were X Men or part of the expanded Fantastic Four. Sorry, none of us can violate physical laws.

As expected, the New Mexico locals became suspicious within a few weeks, so I took the direct approach and called Ray Guiterrez, the New Mexico governor. After a quick explanation of the benefits that our little colony would bring to Debaca and Chaves counties and New Mexico as a whole, we had no more obstruction. The grants to education, the much increased tax base and the prospect of the biggest scientific and cultural centers in the US were all he needed to hear. As expected, he checked with Wilkie to confirm my story.

The cat was out of the bag. Jodi decided to call President Hanley to get ahead of the story. It was our good luck that Duke Hanley had replaced President Burton.

Burton was something of a likeable buffoon, but Hanley was about as smart as any of the unevolved.

Jodi: "Mr. President, I'm so happy that you took my call."

Duke: "I should be honored to be talking to one of the evolved. Call me Duke."

Jodi: "OK. First, what do you know about the evolved?"

Duke: "I think that you are like the children of Einstein, Schwarzenegger, and the Dalai Lama, due to the effects of The Bombardment to your DNA.

Jodi: "A little fanciful, but a good short description. Does the government have a policy towards us?"

Duke: "I'm leaning towards benign negligence. Maybe your New Mexico colony can lead the way to worldwide peace and prosperity."

Jodi: "As long as there are the unevolved, that won't happen, but maybe we could help a little. So, you would not disturb the colony or the evolved that choose to live outside of New Mexico?"

Duke: "That is correct."

Jodi: "Thank you so much, I'm so glad we got this straight. If you don't mind, I'll sign off for now, but I hope that we will stay in touch."

Duke: "I forgot to ask, are you the leader of the evolved?"

Jodi: "We don't have a leader. Any one of us could have called you."

Duke: "My assistant will get back to you on how to keep clear communication. Signing off on this end for now."

Public reaction

A few days later as the evolved went about their work, the phone rang and Sam Hawkins answered because he was closest.

"Hello, this is Jonas Atkins of Flocks News. To whom am I speaking?"

"This is Sam Hawkins."

"Are you the leader of the evolved?"

"We don't have leaders."

"Is this some sort of cult or new religion?"

"No, just a bunch of people trying to improve the human condition."

"If it is not too private, what kind of sex goes on there?"

"Consensual and age appropriate."

"Could you tell me anymore, our audience is intrigued?"

"I'll explain it if you tell us all about the sex practices of the unevolved."

"What are your politics and religion?"

"We don't have any."

"Who does the work and who runs things?"

"When something needs to be done, somebody does it."

"Well, thanks for your time."

We evolved didn't know it because we didn't follow news programs, but Jonas Atkins' next news program "What You Need To Know Now" spent all of its runtime exposing the evolved colony as "A godless conspiracy much like Jonestown or the Rajneeshpuram."

Attack

In response to the program, a militia of thousands organized and attacked the colony. Some hated anything that they didn't understand, some loved violence, and some wanted spoils. I'm not surprised that they confused the intelligent with the defenseless. We tried not to kill anybody.

The siege of The Colony didn't last long because we had put dug a deep moat on our border. Most of the invaders gave up on encountering it and left muttering and swearing.

A few jumped in and some drowned largely because of the shock of the cold water. Sometimes low tech works just fine. Our housing was far enough away from the moat that few tried to fire in our direction and those that did didn't hit anything. For the few that did get across, the electrical grid encouraged them to retreat to the other side of the moat.

We were accused of being barbarians by some in the media. It was suggested that we should jointly be charged with murder for the thirteen deaths. The local authorities wouldn't do anything to us, partly based on legal principle and partly due to the benefits we brought to New Mexico. President Hanley was one our biggest fans, so he had no interest in pursuing any legal action against us. He went further and apologized for not stopping the invaders before they got to our colony.

The program

After that interruption we proceeded with our plan to improve the state of humanity. We were in continuous contact with other evolved colonies around the world, but it wasn't necessary, because we all reached the same conclusions.

The ways in which we could help the world:

> Move non-combatants from war zones. Nothing could be done for those that insist on fighting and we didn't want to "destroy the village in order to save it". There are very few areas which could easily absorb more people. Canada, Australia and Siberia are the major candidates. In each case we had to work on infrastructure and housing plus sources of food and water.

> Produce reliable, renewable and adequate energy for the world. While looking for other solutions, we

installed wind, solar, tidal and thermal plants where needed. Each solution depended on improvements that our best minds produced.

Raise the standard of living for those that need it most. Getting the noncombatants out of war zones was a part of the solution. Our energy projects helped the standard of living in two ways, the most obvious being the availability of heat, cooling, stove and lights and the less obvious is access to education and knowledge from the internet. Evolved volunteers became a "super peace corps" going wherever they were needed and accepted to aid in local projects.

Stabilize the world population. This was our most difficult goal because of the cultural and demographic problems involved. Japan and much of Europe had declining populations, but we concentrated on those areas with unsupportable demographics. For any jurisdiction that would accept it, we offered birth control services.

Educate Women. This is closely related to stabilizing the world population. Women who know more are less like to be baby factories dominated by men and they can improve their local economy.

With the idea that we would introduce these programs where they were accepted, they were quickly introduced to parts of Africa, South America, and Asia. Europe, Canada, Japan and Australia did not need major changes. The difference between the adopters and the resisters was that adopters were largely interested in improving their lot, and the resisters did not want any changes to their culture. In the US, changes were delayed because of an anti-intellectual bent, resistance to birth control and dislike of change. Further, many thought The Colony was a dangerous cult.

Five Years Later

With the very important help of some benevolent billionaires around the world, we have made some progress. Many areas have reliable water and power for the first time. Small, portable houses that supply much of their own energy are being constructed in many parts of the world. Using local materials and labor has simultaneously increased gainful employment and improved housing. Women are running businesses and having fewer, healthier children in many parts of the world.

The parts of the world that resisted us are, if anything, worse off, mired in war, overpopulated and sinking economically. We can only hope that they will eventually see our successes, and learn from them. Even we evolved are stumped in our attempts to deal non-violently with the entrenched intransigence of the medieval cultures in much of the world, but he US is slowly adopting some of our ideas.

The Future

Our daughter Jeanie is now three years old and intellectually equivalent to a teenager but without the hormonal mood swings. She and the other children of the evolved are the hope of the future.

The coming years hold so much promise.

This story was originally serialized in *Swings & Roundabouts*. It is now in *Down In The Dirt*.

The Dumb

Crazy Ed Mahoney went out the back door on Monday to urinate in his garden. He believed, incorrectly, that he was saving on his water bill. His neighbors had given up on changing his ways. After seeing him in the act a few times, they learned not to look in the direction of his backyard at 7am, 1pm and 4pm when Ed would urinate on schedule. Whatever else was wrong with Ed, he had an excellent prostate.

Before Ed had gone ten feet, he hit something invisible and was knocked out. By the time he regained consciousness, most of Clinton Hills had learned of what became known as the Enclosure, which kept Clinton Hills isolated from the outside world, and the outside world out of Clinton Hills.

It was only by chance that no people or animals were injured by the Enclosure, but the Clitters, as local residents were known, panicked at the thought of running out of oxygen. Professor Higgins from their local community college estimated, based on the volume of the Enclosure, the number of residents and their degree of obesity, that the Clitters would suffocate on Ash Wednesday. When he delivered his calculations to the assembled Clitters, a voice from the audience yelled, "Hey, big dome, haven't you noticed the wind blowing through the walls of the Enclosure?"

Higgins thought, *Oh shit*, but said, "I answered the question put to me – how long will we live if deprived of oxygen." He left for his 3pm class at Clinton CC. The town later learned that not only could oxygen come through the membrane, it kept out pollution and the weather was always fine in the Enclosure.

Clitters were only relieved for a few minutes, but then troubled again. The assembled crowd mumbled for a few minutes. No one could tell what anyone else said because

93

of all of the background noise, so you'd have to call it mumbling. Sick of the mumbling, a single voice boomed, "Yeah, but what do we eat?"

Amid the lesser background noise, a few voices were heard:

"Beats me."

"How the hell should I know?"

"The government will fix it."

After an ensuing silence of thirty-four minutes another voice was heard, "It just came to me. Obscure Surveys listed Clinton Hills as the number one town in several categories. We have the most complete agricultural mix of any city in the US with under 25,000 people and the largest store of canned food by paranoid survivalists. I'll bet that we can survive for as long as necessary the way we are set up."

Voices from the multitude responded:

"You know I think that he's right."

"I've got the munchies now."

"I've got an oversupply of zucchinis, broccoli and cauliflower.

"With our hops crop and our local micro Exterminator Stout, I'm not worried."

Local car salesman, dope dealer and Mayor Larry Large decided it was time to take over. "With those two worries taken care of, don't worry about a thing. I'm in charge"

A stranger in town, Carroll Jenkins, listened, but did not speak. He commanded attention merely by his stoic countenance and his insistence that Carroll spelled as it was is a man's name.

As the crowd dispersed, an attractive woman caught Carroll by the arm and said, "You are too good looking to be from here. Who are you?"

"I'm just a man who came to see the world-famous Clinton Tower and happened to kill a man who wanted to steal my billfold while I was sleeping. Name is Carroll, but not spelled like a woman's name."

"Hi I'm Teri, spelled T-e-r-i. Did the guy you killed happen to have hair colored like a skunk and favor Bermuda shorts?"

"Yes, why?"

"It was probably my husband. No loss, he was a dick. Saves me a divorce. But since you cost me a husband, maybe you can do husband things for me."

"Works for me."

Many of the Clitters did not like the highhanded way that Larry Large led Clinton Hills after the Enclosure arrived. Larry knew that one thing that couldn't be produced locally was petrol and he cleverly cornered the market on horses, and charged extravagant prices for them, which resembled the way he did business as a car dealer. His institution of red sock Thursday and banning Taco Tuesday further irritated town folks.

Most of the populace didn't care because Larry did supply marijuana at reasonable rates and kept beer prices low.

Those that did object to Larry gathered around handsome stranger Carroll. One thing that Carroll had in his favor was that Carroll started Orgy Wednesday. It was held at Town Hall and not only attracted enthusiastic participants, but the gallery was always full of observers cheering them on. The town physical therapist was kept busy.

The town was on the edge of a showdown between the Carroll and Larry forces when Larry and Carroll, the only owners of walkie-talkies, got a message.

"This is Senator Biggle. I'm happy to announce we have learned how to open the Enclosure. First a little background. The Enclosure idea was a joint effort of the Army, Monsanto and aliens from the planet Alpha Romeo. The trial Enclosure should have been five meters across in your town square, but Exterminator Stout was spilled on the work order and it was read as five kilometers. Our bad. Here is what you do. Mix up some window cleaner and Coca Cola and spray it where you want an exit. We can't do it out here; it only works from the inside. Keep your walkies on, it is the only way we can contact you."

Larry and Carroll called a truce to decide what to do. They imagined what it would mean to open the Enclosure.

"Federal, state and local taxes."

"No more public orgies, or dope smoking in public."

"Our out-of-town relatives can visit."

Larry and Carroll turned off their walkies.

Published in *Literally Stories*

Gate

"Now that you've been in Ambrosia for a week Sally, what do you think of the place?"

"It definitely exceeds my expectations, Duke, but I still have a few questions."

"Shoot."

"I don't know if I was imagining it, but I met a guy named Henderson who seemed normal, and then the next day I saw the same person with no legs in a wheelchair. Am I imagining things, or are they twins?"

"Neither. Henderson is one of the people that we recruited to join us at no charge. We saw a human interest in the newspaper about him that said he was a big-time volunteer in spite of his handicap. He was very good in his job on a suicide hotline. We were very impressed that despite his handicap, he didn't brood, but did what he could to rescue people in despair. When you saw him out of his wheelchair, he was using prostheses that we have developed. When you saw him later, we were fine tuning his robotic legs. He thinks that we're helping him, but he's also advancing our technology, so both sides win."

"Most of the people that I see here are the makers and shakers, the leaders in business, science and politics. How many of the residents are exceptions like Henderson?"

"I don't have the numbers on me, but something like a third of the residents aren't rich or famous, they are just great humans. We have enough money here, so we can afford to offer places to people who have earned in ways other than money."

"One thing that I like about the place is the evening dance. Some of the residents do a detailed routine, while others just get to free-form."

"They do whatever they feel. I noticed that you are a

truly impressive dancer, Sally. Were you a professional dancer before your time in the WNBA?"

"I had trained from an early age to be a ballerina, but when I reached 5'10" as a fourteen-year-old, I knew that I'd be too big for the danseurs nobles to handle. I was fortunate that I was a good basketball player, so I still had something at which I could excel. Even though I gave up the idea of ballet, I kept up with several dancing disciplines as well as yoga and gymnastics."

"Want to hear a funny story about the dance? You know that because we are so secretive and well-guarded, and have so many famous people here, someone is always trying to get in to find out what we are up to. One evening while we were doing the dance, I saw someone inside the perimeter hiding in the bushes. When we caught him, we warned him that he would be prosecuted if he ever revealed our exotic dancing. I told him that we have the best lawyers in the world and besides those that live here; we have friends in very high places. He was convinced to keep his mouth shut, but the irony is that if he reported what he saw, we'd still come out fine. We had to make some changes to our security system."

"Based on my time here, I can see what you mean. On the subject of the residents, Ambrosia recruited me. You said that you have others that you invite in for various reasons. Does anyone ever apply to get in?"

"Many have. They usually fail. Not too long ago, we had a losing billionaire presidential candidate who expected no problem joining us. He already had plans for adding a casino. Absolutely no one here supported him."

"Do you have any trouble keeping out the undesirables?"

"I mentioned the best lawyers. It helps that we have every single religious, ethnic and sexual orientation here. Every time someone has tried to sue us to join, we have been able to show that the plaintiff is rejected based on being an abhorrent person."

"You mentioned sexual orientation. When I was interviewed, I mentioned that I am polyamorous and love diverse partners. At the time I thought that it might be a deal breaker. Obviously, that was before I learned more about Ambrosia."

"I don't know if you noticed, but when you were interviewed, you were given freedom to just tell about yourself. Our lawyers made sure we didn't ask any question that could open us to legal action. You must have volunteered information about your sexual interests."

"That I did. I wanted to do full disclosure."

"I was told that your father, Duke Sr. started Ambrosia thirty-two years ago."

"Was it thirty-two years? I haven't kept track, but that sounds about right. I believe that he was the world best geneticist, and the Nobel Committee agreed. His advances were astounding, and the outside world doesn't even know about his greatest accomplishments. I was a teenager when we moved in here. I've attempted to make modest headway on his greatest works."

"Oh Duke, don't be modest. I've seen and even experienced some of your best work."

"What do you mean?"

"Henrietta, the one with tentacles, and I got intimately acquainted one evening. If an outsider had seen that, the place would be shut down fast."

"That is why we only play with our designer friends indoors. I'm glad that you enjoyed her company. The darling is as friendly as a Labrador retriever. I hope that you get to enjoy some of the other genetically modified associates that live here. You might be surprised that some of our residents never play with them."

99

"It takes all kinds. I don't judge."

"One last question for now. Do you play requests? I'd like to get close to something with fur."

"That is our next project. I think that it will be a 2020 model. If you put in your request now, it can come with tentacles. Our creatures are the second favorite thing at Ambrosia."

"The first?"

"Brunch."

Published in *Scarlet Leaf* and *Written Tales*

Prime 6

JULIE COLLINS: For our sixth interview with Dook, our Angwin / Yeti spokesman, we are shaking it up. Dook is joined by our first appearance of a female Angwin, Sally.

Before I take questions from the audience, the ushers will pass around a salad made by the Angwin.

OK, first question. Please give your name and where you live. You in the third row, red hat.

JANE: Hi, I'm Jane from Manchester England. Sally, if I'm pronouncing that right, who runs your people, the males or the females?

SALLY: You aren't pronouncing it right, but I've never been able to do French right, so no problem.

We are fairly equalitarian. Unlike humans, we don't have any "male" or "female" jobs, except that females are the baby makers. Females may have the edge when it comes to art, and males for tool making, but the difference is insignificant. The makeup of our councils is fairly evenly split.

JULIE COLLINS: Let's hear from the man in the seventh row with the purple coat.

JAKE MBENGA *from Capetown*: We've heard a lot lately about politicians and celebrities accused of rape or assault on women. Does that happen among the Angwin?

DOOK: Much like humans, Angwin men would like to live a long life, so no.

SALLY: It happens, but it is rare for the reason the Dook gives.

If I may ask a follow up, why is that?

DOOK: I'd like to say that we are an enlightened people. That is true. It is also true that the Angwin women are

101

usually larger and stronger than the men. This is true in most animals, but not among most mammals. We don't know why it is true for the Angwin.

JULIE COLLINS: Let's hear from the man in the Dude hat wearing an orange jacket.

DOUG HAWLEY *from Lake Oswego, Oregon, USA*: In earlier interviews, Dook mentioned that Angwin live in caves and under the snow. Is it one or the other or both?

SALLY: Dook and I chuckled about that earlier. It is both. We apologize for the lack of clarity. Dook made a mistake in suggesting it was primarily one or the other.

JULIE COLLINS: The woman with the red hair and killer dress in row six.

MICHELLE DUVAL *from Lyon, France*: Sally, how were you chosen to be a part of this interview?

SALLY: Same as Dook, short straw. *Audience titters.* Well, that was part of it, but the same as Dook, my English is good and I am knowledgeable in Angwin culture.

JULIE COLLINS: Petite woman in Hello Kitty outfit, tenth row.

MIU FURINGO *Tokyo*: I'm studying to be an environmental engineer and I appreciate the Angwin's dedication to sustainability. How do you handle sewage and refuse?

SALLY: I'll take that because Dook seems to be sleeping or meditating. We generate very little waste, because we don't wear clothing, except for this interview – the producer insisted that we cover the naughty bits – and don't use packaging. Much like humans, we don't eat the yellow snow.

(Chuckling from audience)

Anyway, as you probably know, drinking urine causes no problems.

JULIE COLLINS: Let me interrupt a moment. Did you get "naughty bits" from a Monte Python routine?

DOOK: That's right. The retrogrades have been sending up episodes. Are they making any more episodes?

JULIE COLLINS: Sorry to say that one of the Pythons is deceased and the group doesn't perform together any more. Sorry for the interruption, what were you about to say?

SALLY: As a part of our sustainable practices, solid waste is used in our hydroponic gardens where we grow our vegetables.

How do you like your salads? Spitting and groaning sounds from the audience.

Oh come on, we've been eating this stuff for hundreds of years and no one ever got sick.

JULIE COLLINS: I see that most of the audience is heading for the doors, so that concludes our sixth and last exclusive Angwin interview.

Published in *Occulum*

Reprieve

It started in January of 1990, but the exact date is unknown. George Bush was the US president. The Soviet Union was disintegrating and its satellite states were going their own way. African American politicians experienced mixed success – David Dinkins was elected mayor of New York City and Marion Barry was arrested in Washington DC. A bright light was the beginning of *The Simpsons* on Fox TV.

The world was experiencing its normal quota of evil and not exactly evil.

No one knew it then, but cyanic had left Africa months ago. What made cyanic different from other plagues was that it had an extremely long latency period during which it was communicable, but showed no symptoms. The public had no idea how far the disease had spread until most of the world had been infected. By the time the disease was understood, there was no treatment and most people were doomed.

The first symptom of cyanic was a slightly blue tinge to the skin, hence the scientific name. Most people referred to the victims as "having the blues." Within a week of the color change people started to act like the zombies from the George Romero films and lost cognitive function. Later research found that cyanic hit the higher brain functions first. Unlike movie zombies, cyanics had no taste for brains, or for any food. They just shambled pointlessly until they died.

Researchers determined that cyanic was spread by skin-to-skin contact. A grim humorist was quick to start the "Six degrees of cyanics" game. No one affected was amused.

Pundits noted that it was a case of life imitating art. There were comparisons to Captain Trips in Stephen King's The Stand and the Wandering Disease in the old movie "Shape of Things" based on the works of H.G. Wells.

As usual, before the disease hit its stride, there were the usual conspiracy theories. Jews were blamed, because Jews are blamed for everything. It didn't hurt that the Israelis were less affected than other areas. Sunnis blamed the Shias, the Shias blamed the Sunnis. Before being decimated, there was even more Moslem on Moslem violence than usual. Survivalists saw black helicopters everywhere. Some Christians saw it as God's judgment on secular society and homosexuality in particular. A minority of the people believed the scientists' explanation that cyanic arose as a mutation of the Ebola virus. The explanation was particularly derided by those who did not believe in evolution at all.

The more serious also played the blame game. Environmentalists said in essence "I told you so" as did the anti-immigration people. Those from the more rabid animal rights groups said it was fair because we had been exploiting non-human animals for far too long. A man who had predicted the demise of humans in the next hundred years admitted to being a little optimistic.

Some of those who were exposed had natural immunity. Some, particularly isolated farmers, did not come in contact with the affected. At the other end, large cosmopolitan cities were affected the worst. All of the major world capitals were depopulated. Second tier cities and the "flyover" cities did much better. Portland Oregon, Salt Lake City, Kansas City, Des Moines, Knoxville and Pittsburg fared relatively well.

As the enormity of the plague became clear, disposal teams were organized. Huge pits were dug and crews in hazmat suits herded walking cyanics into them.

The plague started to subside after a few months and eventually stopped. The cause of cyanics died or mutated again. By that time most of the world's population had died. By then the estimated world population had decreased from over five billion to well under a billion. Asia, Africa and South America were particularly hard hit, but no continent had over a quarter of its previous population.

Aside from the horror, life was horrible and wonderful. There were huge stores of food, petrol, cars, appliances and homes that inundated the remaining humans. As expected, liquor and appliance stores were looted. Because the world militaries and governments were disproportionately depleted, people could just take what they wanted. Eventually most people decided that there was little point in having five cars and three houses, and shared reasonably. This was after a few more million had died fighting over the spoils. As always, a few thought that they deserved more, but there were no more African women walking ten miles to get water – the survivors just moved closer to the water, since there was no one there to chase them off. Various means in different communities were used to distribute desirable possessions of the departed. In some places lotteries were used. In other places, it was whoever got there first.

In most of the world, the remaining people gathered around city states and tribes. Such arbitrary borders in Belgium, the Middle East and much of Africa evolved over time. Ethnic minorities in Asia went their own way. China split into five different regions that didn't acknowledge the others' existence. English speaking North America formed a very loose confederation. A minor surviving official in the US claimed that he was the ruler, but was totally ignored. The worldwide partitioning was much easier than the Pakistan – India split years earlier.

The loosely knit North America included Columbia consisting of the Northwest, Alaska, British Columbia and Northern California. It resembled Ecotopia in an old novel. A major product was cannabis. Mexicali consisted of

Southern California, Nevada, Arizona, New Mexico and some of West Texas. The rest of Texas never got reorganized. Vast portions of the Canadian and US plains became Range. US upper Midwest states and Ontario became, after much debate, Lake Land, although some chose to call it Heart Land. Louisiana, Utah, Florida, Quebec and Colorado retained much of their original boundaries. The South not a part of something else went back to Dixie. What was left of the US and Canada became New England.

The regions differed on abortion, minimum wage, anti-discrimination, but had no national authority to overturn their decrees. Utah at least tacitly accepted polygamy, but not same-sex marriage. Most of the former North America did the opposite.

These quasi-governmental areas evolved over a number of years and made a lot more sense than the original state and province boundaries.

Because of the fear of new plagues and a desire for self-sufficiency there was much less trade than before. The former Soviet Union and the Middle East suffered greatly when the demand for gasoline and natural gas dropped like a rock in sync with the population. A positive side effect was that there wasn't enough money to buy hordes of weapons. The major weapons exporters had quit manufacturing anyway. There was some minor scuffling over petty grievances and the need for arable land, but mostly people just moved to their own kind and found a way to feed themselves.

There were a few years when most people didn't worry about work or how to survive. Car breaks down? Get a new one. Need food? Go to the grocery store and take whatever canned food you want. Don't like your home? Move into a new one.

There were some occupations that were still necessary.

Farmers had to grow food, trains and truckers were needed to move things, and people needed to operate utilities. With the much lower need for food, some farmers quit and moved to town, others continued as they had and some moved from marginal land to more fertile areas. In some cases, people who got bored just picked up some of the required jobs. Jack Wiggins in London didn't see any need to be a corporate lawyer, so he started being a railroad engineer. He was lucky not to kill anyone, but eventually he got the hang of it.

At the end of the plague, the largest cities in the North America were Calgary, Indianapolis and Portland OR in that order. All had a little over a hundred thousand people. Calgary continued to be the energy center, Indianapolis evolved into the lead manufacturing site, and Portland moved from being a minor player in entertainment and electronics to the leader in the Americas. The previously major cities were ghost towns.

Zero population adherents were pleased by the lower number of humans, if not how it had happened. Some traditional male Catholics, Muslims and Mormons saw the situation as an opportunity to dominate the world by rapid reproduction. The women were not as enthused.

Energy production and pollution were greatly reduced by much smaller use of the energy sources. For a while a lot of people wanted to get the biggest Suburbans, Land Cruisers, Rolls, Bentleys and Mercedes they could find, but that got old after a while. The energy needs of earth were scaled down roughly in proportion to the population drop. An added advantage was that there were plenty of sources for energy without using the more polluting forms such as coal.

Because entertainers and producers didn't have much need for money and the stars were mostly deceased, local talent and local no talent took over television, radio and the stage. The results were mixed. There were Paul Newmans and Meryl Streeps who simply hadn't been discovered, as well as Joe Plum, who had a post-plague, short-lived TV show in which he talked about his coin collection. There were all porn channels, golf channels, romance channels, run by amateurs or low-level professionals. Janet Levitz from the Bay Area and Thane Gibbons, a Portland native, wandered into the mix. Their bright idea, concocted and run in Portland, was InVid, a video sharing service.

David Nelson Hilliard was intrigued by InVid. He saw it as his way to become a star. After he recalled that he had no talent, he revised his thinking to believe that he would become a world leader. To say that he had a Napoleonic complex would be an insult to Napoleon. His lack of looks was compensated for by his lack of height. He was, however, a forward thinker and saw a way to profit from the new world order and even attract some girls. After a few hours of intense work, he had a plan to rule the world.

The next day he had his tall dark and handsome neighbor Doug record the Hilliard Manifesto on InVid as well as calling as many world state leaders as possible.

"New Earth arises from Old Earth tested and improved. From this, the worst tragedy in human history, we gain our reprieve from impending disaster. For if the plague had not wiped out much of the earth's human population, we would have soon done the job ourselves. Deforestation, ocean acidification, global storming, overpopulation, mass human caused extinctions and pollution were the stepping stones to human extinction.

"Now we have to ask, will we repeat the same mistakes? I say no and I have a program to give us a few million more years of dominion on planet earth. The United Nations died with the pre-plague earth. Let us start a new organization consistent with the new reality. I propose World Harmony.

"The states in World Harmony will agree to:

Assist neighbors in need if able;

Refrain from acts of aggression against our neighbors or supporting a national army;

Allow immigration if economically practical;

Allow emigration;

Support World Harmony Armed Forces;

Assist in the defense of states under attack and

Obey the decisions of the World Court;

"After joining World Harmony, states may be expelled by the World Court.

"National leaders may wonder what advantage you might gain from membership in World Harmony. You will get protection from aggressive neighbors and assistance in an emergency. The price that you pay is fairly small."

For months there was no response. Then there was a trickle of positive responses. After a couple of years most of the post-plague nations had signed up. Some of them remembered the United Nations as a positive, if not perfect institution and wanted a replacement. Others liked the simple set of rules. A number of states didn't like their existing borders, and decided to stay out.

As the instigator, Hilliard set himself up as the first Governor of World Harmony in 1995. The headquarters was in an abandoned bank in downtown Portland. The World Court was organized the following year. The member states formed World Harmony military bases on each continent.

In 1997 World Harmony was tested for the first time. The minor states of the former Burma – Kachin, Karen,

Muslim Region and others – were attacked by the majority Burmese state, Myanmar. World Harmony forces from Mumbai were able to restore order and expel Myanmar from World Harmony; with the promise that Myanmar could reapply for admission after proving that it had disbanded its illegal army. Thereafter, World Harmony was taken seriously.

Post-plague earth went along fat and happy for a few years using up the assets left over from before the plague. Governor Hilliard, in particular was fat and happy. His status had indeed gotten him girls or women – those with low esteem and those that wanted to get close to power. His favorite was Rose Reed, who knew how to flatter and please him. Just as some say you can't cheat an honest man, manipulators are often manipulated. In June of 1999 Jacque Braque of New France called Hilliard and suggested they were living on borrowed time. It was fortunate that Braque spoke better English than Hilliard did.

"Governor Hilliard, you have done a great job so far, keeping the world peace. However, we have serious challenges ahead of us. At some point the old cars, appliances will break down, utilities will need maintenance and housing will fall apart. Something else that you may not be aware of, many computers will fail in January because they will not recognize the year 2000. Not only do we have a challenge, we have an opportunity; we can improve on our lives compared to before the plague. We have the chance for a do over."

Now Hilliard wasn't smart and he didn't understand the implications of what Braque had said. Hilliard thought everything was fine because he had the love (or so he thought) of several resourceful and beautiful women, all he could eat and drink and the admiration of millions. He was, however, manipulative and lazy.

"Mr. Braque, you and I are entirely in sync. I was just saying to an assistant today, we need to plan for the future. The name that came up repeatedly to head up the effort was yours. Consider that you have a blank check written by me to plan for the future."

"Thank you, Governor. I already have tentative plans."

Hilliard immediately put out the word that his assistant would be implementing Hilliard's plan to improve the world's future.

Braque knew that Hilliard would want all the credit, but was willing to proceed anyway.

In Braque's mind engineering was the easy part, politics was the hard part. Towards that end, he asked for planners and engineers from all of the world's states. After interviewing them, he knew which to use and which to work around. Whichever category they fell in, the contributions of all of them and their states would be highly praised.

After a get-to-know-you party for all of them, he outlined his plans.

"As you all know we are currently living on credit. We can have a bright future or fall into darkness. It is up to us.

"My plan:

> Those who live in dangerous places subject to flooding, hurricanes, drought or monsoons should move to safer available places.

> Fishing and forestry must be sustainable. In fact, our forests and fish stocks must be replenished.

> We should move to renewable energy sources such as tidal, solar and wind. I depend on all of you here to do the research and building as necessary.

> Vehicles should be made to be practical and run by either electricity or something better if we can come

up with it. As much as possible, they should be recyclable.

Each region should be self-sufficient. If this is impractical in some cases, we should provide assistance as necessary.

We must avoid overpopulation, which was part of the cause of the plague.

Rivers should run free and with the depopulation, there should be huge animal reserves. Threatened African wildlife and buffalos in the US can make a comeback.

"I know that there will be resistance to these ideas in some quarters. 'What about my house at the shore? Will I still have a cell phone?' There may be some sacrifices, but I think that we can sell a better future, and yes you can still have a cell phone. If you have a house at the coast, no one will insure it. So before we start, you have to sell the plan to your people, if indeed you are on board.

"Questions or comments?"

"Yes Ms. Sebastian of Chile?"

"Your plan sounds good, but what benefits will my country get?"

"Correct me if I'm wrong, but I believe that your country imported crude oil before the plague and now you are having difficulty obtaining supplies. We want you to be able to produce your own energy and fuels indigenously."

"Mr. Kralic of Bosnia?"

"Will your government people interfere with our customs or government?"

"Depends on what you mean. In general, no. If your state should produce an unsustainable population, or over exploit your resources, you will not be in the program and you will not be receiving our assistance. Is that clear?"

"All too clear."

"Now if you would, we have arranged for all of you to join tables with facilitators to answer your questions and take your comments."

After several hours and bathroom, snack and drink breaks, the state leaders left with a fairly clear idea of what Mr. Braque's plan was. Most were in favor, but there were a few dissenters. The somewhat diminished China was not sure about blowing up its major dams. The North America Columbia region was ambivalent about losing the dams that provided most of the region's electricity.

Mr. Braque had his engineers draw up scenarios for the dissenters showing how they would come out ahead by moving their constituents to safer areas, letting rivers and forests return to their state before the industrial revolution, and replacing coals burning power plants by solar, wind and tidal power. They also showed how much the energy needs would be decreased by some simple changes, for example replacing much of the heating and cooling of houses by circulating water underground and then back through the houses. Most of the world states bought it. Some that distrusted anything smacking of Western culture were hold outs.

With most of the world on board, Braque made a five-year timeline for what he was convinced was a way to keep the planet going for a long time. The next few years would see a modest beginning to a lessening of the extinction of flora and fauna and pollution.

The first step, replacing computer legacy programs before the year 2000 was easier than expected.

Rose was immediately attracted to Jacque's intelligence and looks, particularly compared to Hilliard. The only thing that Jacque was missing was Hilliard's power. She made sure that they bumped into each other, literally in some cases, from time to time. Jacque, whose wife had died in the plague, was interested.

The morning after meeting in a local motel, they discussed the future. They had been too busy to talk the night before.

"Tell me, Rose, how that buffoon could become the most powerful man in the world? His World Harmony idea looks like it was taken from a cereal box, or an episode of GI Joe."

"I think it was a Cheerios box. He had three things going for him. He got the timing right. He had a feel for attracting the right people. He is a master manipulator. Oh yeah, four things – he was incredibly lucky."

"Are you satisfied being his number one consort?"

"Hell no; it was just the best deal I could make at the time. I admit it; I was looking for my main chance. You tell me something. Are you happy letting somebody you call a buffoon treat you as his lowly assistant?"

"As you say, hell no."

"I know with certainty that Hilliard will die in the next few months, are you ready to plan for his exit?"

"How do you know that, Rose?"

"You're better off if you don't know. Here is my question for you Jacque: are you ready to take over World Harmony with me? I've already arranged to be married to him before he dies; that will give us some legitimacy from the get go."

"I can't think of a better team than you and I. How do you know he will marry you?"

"He's so insecure. I just told him I'd leave if he didn't. When he is gone, after a reasonable mourning period, we get married. Our ascension will be almost a coronation. I've already lined up support within the government. I've been running several departments for months. Can you get your engineering staff behind you?"

"Easy."

Fifty days after this conversation Hilliard was dead. As

Reed had indicated, taking over was easy. Hilliard had been seen as a figurehead for at least a year, and people were used to working with Reed and Braque. Their marriage a month after Hilliard's death sealed the deal.

A decade later there were clear improvements in land, sea and air. Many formerly endangered species were thriving. There were few conflicts between modern conveniences and the ecology. The world population had only increased only 2% since the plague. There were a few local conflicts, but nothing major. Reed and Braque had a son and a daughter, who were in training to run the world when the time was right. In a self-congratulatory mood, Rose said to Jacque, "I was thinking we should declare a Thousand Year Reich, but that might not sound right."

"Right, but we should get our PR people to work on that, see what they can come up with."

"It is hard for to believe how this has turned out for me. I was always smarter than the other guys, but people only paid attention to my body. That's where Hilliard screwed up. If he had given me more credit, he might still be around."

"I had it tough too. I was always scorned as the French version of a nerd. Nobody wanted to hear me talk about anything except other scientists. If she'd lived longer, my wife would have left me."

"And here we are at the head of a dynasty."

The phone rang.

After listening for a while, Reed blanched. When she hung up, she said, "This is very bad."

"I couldn't be worse that what we've been through the last ten years."

"It could and it is. An asteroid is heading towards earth."

Published multiple times from 2015 when pandemic fiction wasn't cool, including by Bridge House in *Covid 19: An Extraordinary Time*.

Acknowledgements

I'd like to thank all of the publishers who have shown the good sense to publish me. I'll just mention one – Literally Stories, whose editors are a convivial group. My parents Grant and Sue who got this kid started, and sister Alex who wrote first. Maysam Kandej who has supported my writing for many years. A series of cats that have inspired stories. Most of all Sharon, the multi-talented person who has served as my in house editor from the beginning.

I thank also Bridge House, Gill and Martin James, and James Patrick.

About the Author

Doug Hawley was born in Portland Oregon USA into a nuclear (his good fortune – it didn't explode) family of father, mother, and sister. During the time that he went through school, and started teaching math in Morehouse College in Atlanta, nothing outstanding happened. Before his second year at Morehouse he met Sharon who would very quickly become his partner of 52 years and his editor for the last nine. After early retirement from actuarial work, both employed and self-unemployed, he took on a number of volunteer jobs. In 2014 he restarted writing as a consequence of being inspired by local author Cheryl Strayed's story "Wild" and pain in his knees and feet which limited his mobility for about a year. To his amazement, he could be published – currently around six hundred times, including the numerous stories now in defunct publications. Those writings have appeared in England, the USA, Canada, India, Iran, Australia, Spain, Germany, Scotland, and in international journals and are scattered over different lengths, and all of the usual genres of fiction and non-fiction.

Website https://sites.google.com/site/aberrantword/

Blog https://doug.car.blog/

Like to Read More Work Like This?

Then sign up to our mailing list and download our free collection of short stories, *Magnetism*. Sign up now to receive this free e-book and also to find out about all of our new publications and offers.

Sign up here:
    http://eepurl.com/gbpdVz

Please Leave a Review

Reviews are so important to writers. Please take the time to review this book. A couple of lines is fine.

Reviews help the book to become more visible to buyers. Retailers will promote books with multiple reviews.

This in turn helps us to sell more books… And then we can afford to publish more books like this one.

Leaving a review is very easy.

Go to http://bit.ly/3TxZ1Yh, scroll down the left-hand side of the Amazon page and click on the "Write a customer review" button.

Read More of Doug's Work

"Smart Car" (the series) in *Best Of Fiction On The Web*
Published by Charlie Fish, February 2018
Order from Amazon:
 ISBN 978-0-992693-91-6 (paperback)
This first of 32 episodes has been published multiple times
and translated twice.

"Nose"
Published by Literally Stories, March 2018
https://literallystories2014.com/2018/03/19/nose-by-doug-hawley/
Otherworldly transition from the world's worst singer to
the best.

Other Publications by Bridge House

The Day Chuck Berry Died
by Ian Inglis

A collection of eclectic and original short stories that bring into focus those decisive moments in a person's life whose significance may not be recognised at the time, but which often have profound and lasting impacts long into the future.

The distorted contours of human nature, as practised in the daily activities of professional footballers; the repercussions of a young man's visit to the battlefields of Flanders to visit his grandfather's grave; a surprising encounter in a Parisian cafe. Choices made on the basis of what we know – or what we think we know – which come back to torment us, challenge us, enlighten us; attitudes and behaviour we can barely comprehend; routine events and situations that bring with them periods of great sadness or unexpected happiness; confusion and clarity when long-hidden truths are finally revealed.

Order from Amazon:

Paperback: ISBN 978-1-914199-32-5
eBook: ISBN 978-1-914199-33-2

A Feast of Tales (Gently Twisted)
by Dawn Bush

A tempting tale for every mood.

An eclectic mixture of tales that take you to a pragmatic Fairyland, where anything can happen – and not all of it beneficial; to an unknown dusty planet in the distant sky; back in time on earth through time, space, land and sea; through love, selfishness and triumph. They are a feast of the unexpected.

A Feast of Tales (Gently Twisted) is an intriguing collection of short stories by Dawn Bush.

"A charming selection of stories. With some fairy tales and other contemporary stories, there is a mixture of wit and realism. But all beautifully written. Thoroughly recommended." (*Amazon*)

Order from Amazon:

Paperback: ISBN 978-1-914199-12-7
eBook: ISBN 978-1-914199-13-4

I Knew it in the Bath
by Linda Flynn

I Knew it in the Bath is a collection of absorbing short stories which show that no matter how we expect events to unfold, life has a way of confounding us. What will a woman do to save her friend? Do we really know when we're being watched? Why did Dora throw the iron through the window? What's the best way to take revenge on a cheating partner?

Settle back for an engaging read through these humorous, sinister and thought-provoking stories, but try not to drop your book in the bath!

Linda Flynn, a frequent contributor to our annual themed anthologies, gives us food for thought in the stories collected in *I Knew in in the Bath.*

"I can't recommend this anthology enough. Linda Flynn has such a way with words." (*Amazon*)

Order from Amazon:

Paperback: ISBN 978-1-914199-28-8
eBook: ISBN 978-1-914199-29-5